HOW TO KILL A MAN

Books by Tobias Wells

HOW TO
KILL A MAN

TOBIAS WELLS

PUBLISHED FOR THE CRIME CLUB BY
DOUBLEDAY & COMPANY, INC.
GARDEN CITY, NEW YORK
1972

First Edition

Library of Congress Catalog Card Number 71–175405
Copyright © 1972 by Doubleday & Company, Inc.
All Rights Reserved
Printed in the United States of America

*To Doctor Evelyn Parsons
and
Doctor Arthur Baldwin,
a pair of fine physicians*

HOW TO KILL A MAN

I had acquired a new habit. Every morning now, the minute I opened my eyes, I looked across to see if Brenda's head was on her pillow. It began, the new habit, because sometimes I dreamed that I'd lost her. It took the sight of her dark hair against the white pillow-case to reassure me.

I looked now and was reassured. I glanced at the clock on the bedside table. Nearly eight. It was my day off from Station One, Boston Police Department, and I could afford to sleep until eight. I changed position, gave some thought to getting up, and Brenda said, "Good morning, Knute."

"Good morning." I turned to face her. My turncoat tomcat Mein Hair (name by this time shorted to Mein —it was a silly name anyway) stood up on the other side of Brenda, yawned hugely, stretched tall.

Brenda smiled at me. I smiled back. We'd been married three weeks, and I knew now how good it was to have someone smile at you in the morning.

Mein yawned again, meowed in the middle of the yawn. Brenda reached out to pat him. He began to purr like a 747 revving up. "Slob," I said to him.

"What time is it?" asked Brenda. Her bare shoulders were cream colored against the sheets.

I

"Eight on."

She pushed herself up on her elbows and the covers fell back. Her nightgown was pale blue with thin little straps and lots of lace. "I'd better get breakfast started." She laughed. "I feel so deliciously lazy. Like a kept woman."

I pushed my covers back. "Then act like one."

Mein was eating like there was no tomorrow and Brenda and I were drinking coffee when the telephone rang.

Brenda answered it, which was just as well because it was for her. "Why, Antoinette, how nice to hear from you!"

I raised my eyebrows and Brenda made motions that meant she'd tell me later. "What are you doing in Boston?" she asked.

Antoinette, whoever she was, made noises on the end of the line and Brenda said, "Oh, yes, I think I saw something about it in the paper. They're having a convention or something—how long will you be here?"

Antoinette told her two days, I gathered, because Brenda said, "Only two days? Well, I do hope you can find time to come over for dinner."

Mein brushed up against Brenda's legs, agitating for more food. I got up to give him some. Tabby Treat liver and fish, that's all he'll eat these days. Next week it may be something else.

"What about tonight then?" Brenda was saying to Antoinette. "I do so want you to meet Knute."

I grimaced at Mein but he ignored me, stuck his face in his dish.

"Fine." Brenda sounded pleased. "About six will be fine. Do you want us to pick you up? Well, yes, a taxi might be easier if you aren't certain of the time . . . that's wonderful, Antoinette. We'll look forward to seeing you."

"Who?" I asked when she'd hung up.

She grinned saucily. "I told you you'd be sorry if you married me. That's my mother's cousin, my second cousin, Antoinette Evers, one of my million far-flung relatives. Age? Who knows? Maybe sixty—sixty-five. Spinster. And—are you ready? Lady poet."

"Oh, boy." I grinned back at her. "Have I told you about my third cousin Otto? He only works at Christmas, he's a bell ringer. And then there's Great-uncle Leopold. He's taken up six-day bike racing . . ."

"Silly." She poured us more coffee. "Antoinette is a dear old girl, really. I haven't seen her in ages. She couldn't make the wedding, she wrote that she wasn't feeling well. Actually, I was surprised to hear she was in Boston. She sticks pretty close to home which is up-state Vermont."

"What's she doing here?" I got up to let Mein out. "Eat and run," I told him. He gave me a disdainful look and walked out on his balcony. From there, he could survey the harbor before making his way down the fire escape.

3

"It's a convention. The College of Creative Writing, she's an alumnus. You know, that correspondence school for writers? It's advertised in all the magazines."

"I thought that was the Famous Writers School." I swallowed the last of my coffee, reached for the sports page of the paper. The Red Sox were playing five hundred ball. They had to do better than that if they were aiming for the pennant.

"The College of Creative Writing is the other one. Don't know who copied whom, but Antoinette seems devoted to this one. She was as close to gushing as she gets when she told me Arthur Glenn Pendleton was going to be there in person. And Antoinette isn't the gushy type."

Tiger Brown was scheduled to pitch this afternoon, I noted. If I could get a pair of tickets, maybe Brenda would enjoy an afternoon at the ball park. "Arthur Glenn Pendleton? Oh, yeah. The 1970 Hemingway. Want to go to the Red Sox game this afternoon?"

"I'd love to. But would we be back before six?"

"Long before six. Four, four-thirty, it should be over."

And it was. We got home at five and while Brenda fussed with food I fed Mein (again) and then mixed a pitcher of gimlets. "Does Antoinette take a drink?" I asked, measuring vodka.

"Oh, I think so. One, probably. She's kind of mod in her old-lady New England way. Let's see, I'll have a shrimp salad and rolls and maybe some sherbet for dessert.

4

It's almost too warm for a lot of hot food. Does that sound all right to you?"

"Great." I tasted the gimlets, put the pitcher and some glasses in the refrigerator. The telephone rang at the exact moment I closed the refrigerator door. "I'll get it."

Brenda, absorbed in shrimp and lettuce arrangements, nodded.

"Hello."

"Oh! Who's this? Oh. Is this Knute?" It was a woman's voice, a little high and wobbly, like a child's, and uptight.

"Yes, this is Knute Severson. Who's this?"

"Antoinette. Antoinette Evers. Did Brenda tell you . . . ?"

"Yes, she did. We're expecting you. Having trouble finding the place? Just tell the cabbie . . ."

"I didn't know who else to call. They said I could make a phone call and I didn't know . . ."

"Who said you could make a phone call?" I frowned at the telephone.

"The police. They were very careful to explain that they weren't charging me with anything, they just want to question me, but they explained my rights and that includes a phone call."

I waved my hand in Brenda's direction to get her to come listen. "What do the police want to question you about?"

5

"Arthur Glenn Pendleton." The voice cracked, suddenly sounding old. "He's dead, you see, and I was the only one in his suite, I was waiting to talk to him . . ."

"Where are you, Miss Evers?" I kept my voice matter-of-fact to calm her down.

"Where am I?" she asked somebody. Then, "They say I'm at Division One, Station One, that is, near the government center . . ."

"Let me speak to—who's with you?"

Another consultation. "Detective Pinkerton."

"Let me speak to Pinkerton." I'd almost said Pinky. He came on and I said, "This is Knute, Pinky. What's going on?"

"Knute! She didn't say . . . I didn't know who she was calling. This big shot writer is dead, poisoned, we think, and we've got newspaper types coming out of the woodwork and this old—this Miss Evers was right on the scene."

"I'll be right over. Miss Evers is a relative of Brenda's. Tell her I'll be right along."

"Has something happened to Antoinette?" Brenda demanded even before I'd gotten the phone back in its cradle.

I told her and she stared in disbelief. "Antoinette? At Station One?" She picked up her straw bag. "I'm going with you."

"Okay," I said, "but you'd better put that stuff back in

6

the refrigerator or Mein will have himself a shrimp feast by the time we get back."

The place was crawling with newspaper guys and an assortment of people generally described as "coming from all walks of life." Davoren was doing his best to fend off the press and Timmons and Blaisdell were dealing with the assortment. I didn't see Pinkerton and I couldn't tell right off which one was Miss Evers. There was a fat, elderly woman with gray hair hanging straight below her shoulders, she could be it except I didn't think so, and there was a tall, thin woman with a hard mouth and close-set eyes who might be it only I didn't think she was and Brenda confirmed my doubts by whispering, "Where's Antoinette?"

"Knute." Davoren looked surprised. "What are you doing here on your day off?" Captain Granger's clerk wore a more than usually harassed expression.

"Hey, Knute, old buddy, what do you know about this Pendleton thing?" This from Dolph Smith of the Boston *Herald Traveler*. I hardly recognized him, he was without his alpine hat, a winter-summer headpiece, and he'd lost weight.

"Not a thing, Dolph," I answered easily. "Pinkerton around, Davoren?"

"Pinkerton? He's . . ." Davoren got my message and played it cool. "He's down the hall, I think."

7

Down the hall I think meant Pinkerton was in one of the interrogation rooms. I nodded thanks, side-stepped Dolph and his cohorts, grabbed Brenda by the hand and we threaded our way through the wall-to-wall people. A youngish fellow with odd-colored eyes and a sculptured Van Dyke beard was saying to Dracut, "But you don't understand. We have all these people here for two days, dinners have been planned, speakers, seminars. I have to know what's going to happen, I have to tell these people . . ."

Dracut rolled his eyes at me as we passed by and into the comparative quiet of the hall. The door to interrogation one was open, so they weren't in there. Two was closed and I knocked and Pinkerton said, "Come in," and we did.

Pinky, his red hair mussed, sat on one side of the little table and across from him was one of the smallest little old ladies I'd ever seen. She looked almost like a child sitting there, would have looked like a child if it weren't For her yellow-white hair and little wrinkled face. "Antoinette!" Brenda cried and put her arms around her.

Miss Evers patted Brenda's shoulder as though she were the one doing the comforting and turned her little face up to me. "You must be Knute," she said in her piping voice. "Detective first grade Knute Severson. As soon as I knew you were coming I felt absolutely safe. I told this young man that I would answer all his questions when you came." She patted Brenda again and smiled. "So, ask away, young man. I'm ready."

It seemed that Arthur Glenn Pendleton, writer of best sellers and founder of the College of Creative Writing, had checked into the new and ultramodern Tiverton House at about eleven o'clock that morning. He had been given a three-room suite on the twenty-sixth floor, a corner suite with a two-sided view of the new Boston and the Charles River. Accompanying him was his secretary, Derek Pomfret.

The three hundred and eight registered conventioneers had been delegated to floors fourteen and fifteen. Occupying suites on these floors were the executive director of the College of Creative Writing, one G. Harding Fenster; and four instructors, two were women, Dora Elgin and Lois Durant by name, and two were male, Aldrich Towle and Tracy Berg. Also in residence, but suiteless, were Penny Paul, Towle's secretary, and Ann Quigley, who served as an assistant to the instructors.

At this point I interjected, "Six people? Four instructors for three hundred and eight students? That's a pretty high pupil-teacher ratio, isn't it? Seventy-seven students to each instructor."

Antoinette looked pained. "Actually, it's worse than that. I had no idea before I came . . . there are over six hundred currently enrolled in the college. That's one of the things I wanted to speak to Mr. Pendleton about. I told him on the phone, 'I have a bone to pick with you,

sir,' and he said, 'Why, certainly, Miss Evers, any time.'
So I went right down to his suite, or I should say up to
his suite because I'm on the fourteenth floor, but Mr. Pomfret wouldn't let me see him, said I would have to wait
until another time, that Mr. Pendleton was very busy and
I said, 'Very well, then, I'll wait!' Which I did. I'm too
old to be intimidated by glares from a young man hiding
behind a beard."

Beard. Perhaps the Van Dyke in the squad room was
Derek Pomfret. "I thought you told me on the phone you
were the only one in the suite. If Pomfret was there . . ."

"Oh, he went out. He got a phone call, something about
the arrangements for tomorrow night's banquet and he
told me I would have to go, that he had to go down to the
banquet room and see to things, but I said I had no in-
tention of leaving, he'd have to put me out bodily." Her
small face blazed with triumph at the memory.

"And he didn't do that, of course."

"Of course he didn't! He just glared some more and
tugged at his beard. Then he rang Mr. Pendleton's room
from his bedroom, they each had a bedroom and I was in
the third room, the sitting room so I couldn't hear everything Mr. Pomfret said even though I tried. But Mr. Pendleton apparently told Mr. Pomfret to lock him, Mr. Pendleton, in. So right in front of my eyes, Mr. Pomfret locked
the door to Mr. Pendleton's room and took the key. Bold
as brass, he did it, making sure I'd get the message, and
then he left. I had a Parthian shot for him, I can tell you.

I told him I could sit there till doomsday!" She looked suddenly crestfallen. "And I did, didn't I? Till Mr. Pendleton's doomsday."

"Pomfret locked the sitting room entrance to Pendleton's room?" I imaged her sitting implacably and could almost feel sympathy for Pomfret. "What about the connecting door to Pomfret's room? There should have been one."

"The bathroom was between," explained Pinkerton, "and that door was locked, too. Pomfret says Pendleton locked it from inside, one of those turn locks. And apparently he did, because we found it locked all right."

"What was Pendleton doing holed up in his bedroom anyway?" I wondered.

Antoinette sniffed. "After I pinned him down, Mr. Pomfret said he was resting. He said Mr. Pendleton was having his usual nap, that he was exhausted by his trip from California and that he couldn't be disturbed." She gave another sniff. It seemed she took a dim view of grown men who napped in the afternoon.

"So what happened next?"

"I waited. I found a magazine, a copy of *Playboy* with a story by Mr. Pendleton in it. I read that, below his usual standards, I fear, and then I read everything else in the magazine; it's important to know what the markets are using, you know, and *Playboy* does pay awfully well. I was thinking of slanting some of my poetry to them—anyway, when I got through the magazine I looked at my watch and saw it was nearly four o'clock. I knew I should leave the hotel by five or five-thirty, I had no idea how long it would take to get to your place, and I still had to change my clothes so I began to be nervous about the time. I was determined to talk to Mr. Pendleton, after all I'd waited so long already, so I gathered my courage, got up and rapped on his door. 'Mr. Pendleton,' I said, 'it's four o'clock, time you got up, and I must speak to you."

Pinky replied to my unspoken question. "He didn't answer. He couldn't. Doc Albert figures he died around 3 P.M. Miss Evers called the desk, she said she got worried when he didn't answer . . ."

"Not even to say 'go away,' " she put in. "And I knocked pretty hard the second and third time, I can tell you. And shouted."

"The desk sent the floor matron around with a key," Pinky went on, "and she tried the knocking act, too, before she unlocked the door. There was Pendleton, in bed as advertised. But dead."

"Poisoned, you said. What was the poison?"

"Doc Albert wouldn't say."

"Wouldn't say? Or couldn't say?"

Pinkerton shook his head. "He's doing the post-mortem now. Ordinarily, I'd expect he couldn't say. But he looked funny when I put the question to him. I had an idea that he had a hunch but wanted to check it out first."

That was on the odd side, I thought. Poisons come in so many forms that a doctor can hardly tell by looking or even by smelling, unless it's something easy like cyanide that has a distinctive odor. "How do you figure the poison—whatever it was—was administered?"

Pinkerton's reddish eyebrows rose. "By hypodermic needle. I thought you knew."

"By hypodermic?" That was the last answer I'd expected.

"Sure. It was right there on the night table. That's why I figured Doc Albert had a hunch . . ."

"Then you mean, whatever it was, it was self-administered?"

"Well, sure. I mean, it certainly looks that way."

"Drugs," Antoinette piped up. "I'll bet he was hooked on drugs." She looked to Pinky for confirmation.

"I don't think . . . Doc Albert didn't think so . . . I mean, I think he didn't think so." Pinky's answer was more for my benefit than Antoinette's.

I asked her, "Didn't Pendleton make a sound while you sat there? A groan, a call for help, anything?"

She shook her head regretfully. "Not a sound. But then, I think that hotel has excellent soundproofing. Not like some of these places today with walls of paper."

I didn't even know if Pendleton would have cried out, no way of knowing until we knew what he died of, how it would have affected him. Brenda interrupted my thought process by asking, "Then all you need from Antoinette, Miss Evers, is her statement? Supporting the evidence of accidental death?"

"Or suicide," I added.

"I explained that that was all we wanted," Pinkerton told Antoinette.

She drew herself to her full height, which still ended up being short. "I understood. But I feel better with family, with Brenda and her husband here. You never know . . . I'm not used to being involved with the police."

"Pinkerton will have your statement typed up and you'll sign it, that's all," I assured her. "That's the routine. We have to investigate any unexpected death. You're not being accused of anything."

"You never know," she repeated. "They might have thought I was a drug pusher. Suppose I knew no one in town, had no one to testify to my character? They might have gotten the idea that I was the one who brought him the drugs he had in the hypodermic. I live near the Canadian border, you know, they might have thought I smuggled drugs in from Canada . . ."

"There were no drugs involved." Pinky looked exasperated.

"Are you sure? You never know." Antoinette looked smug. "I keep up with things in the world. I've read all about LDS and speed and those things."

"LSD," I corrected her.

"Well, whatever it is. It's not inconceivable that someone like me could be a drug pusher."

Pinkerton looked to me for help. "Go get her statement, Pinky," I advised.

"You'll be able to come to dinner after all," Brenda told Antoinette.

"I certainly hope so," she replied. "I am definitely looking forward to it."

Antoinette was partial to daiquiris, she said, so I mixed a second pitcher while she and Brenda got caught up on the well-being or ill-being of various relatives. Brenda reported on the New Hampshire clan and Antoinette had a good deal to say about her brother Forrest's daughter Doreen who had grown up to be "the prettiest thing you ever saw—big brown eyes and hair like evening sunshine, all red and gold."

"I was terribly sorry you couldn't come to the wedding," Brenda told her as I poured a daiquiri into a frosted glass.

"Oh, I was, too. But I wasn't up to par at the time. It wasn't anything serious, as you can see I've quite recovered. I've been working very hard of late—I've had two poems accepted by *Ponder* Magazine recently and I've just finished something very interesting, a departure for me. Not poetry, exactly, but definitely poetic in feeling . . . I was hoping that Mr. Pendleton might look at it, give me a suggestion as to where to send it, but now . . ."

"Here you are, Antoinette." I served her the daiquiri, handed Brenda her gimlet. "Was this the first time you'd met Pendleton?"

"I don't think you could say I met him at all, could you?" She sipped at her glass. "Uhmmm, this is good. You do make a good daiquiri, Knute. You see I didn't see Mr. Pendleton at all until the maid opened the door."

"He wasn't on hand to welcome the delegates?"

"No. He arrived too late, according to Derek Pomfret, something about his plane being delayed in Chicago. Oh, what a lovely pussy cat. What's her name?"

Mein had entered, posed now in the doorway. "His name is Mein Hair, but we call him Mein."

"Here, kitty, here, Mein." Antoinette reached out with small, thin fingers. "I always think of cats as shes, I don't know why."

"Tell me more about this College of Creative Writing," I urged. "How do you get into it?"

"You've seen the ads, I'm sure. It's a boon for us who live in backwoods areas. At least, I thought it was a boon when I enrolled. It's difficult to find a single soul who shares an enthusiasm for writing up where I live. Most everyone I know lives and dies by the soap opera plots and entertainment for the majority on the television. And as for helpful advice. Well, really! That's why, when I saw the ad, I clipped it out and sent my sample in."

"Sample?" Mein had decided he liked Antoinette. He jumped up on the sofa beside her, turned around and curled up at her side. She stroked him.

"Yes, sample. They want to know if you have any

16

talent, any aptitude, so they ask you to send a short sample of your work which they analyze without charge. Well, when I received the phone call . . ."

"Phone call?"

"Yes, from New York, that's where the college is actually, in New York. It was Mr. Fenster who telephoned. G. Harding Fenster. He said that normally he would have replied by post, but he was so intrigued, that was his word, intrigued by my poem that he'd simply picked up the telephone and called information and rang me up."

I cocked an eyebrow at Brenda. "What happened next?"

Antoinette took another sip of daiquiri. All she seemed to take were sips, yet the glass was almost empty. I made a mental note to refill it shortly.

"He said I simply must enroll. He said I was full of 'raw promise.' And then he told me how much the course cost." She wrinkled her small nose.

"Which was?"

"Nearly a thousand dollars. I could have wept. I said, 'Mr. Fenster, I simply haven't that kind of money, I live on a fixed income, it's out of the question.'"

"Let me get you another daiquiri." I stood up and she gave me her glass. "Go on, I can hear you in the kitchen."

"Well, he sounded almost as disappointed as I was. He talked of monthly payments and such but I was raised to consider credit an absolute evil and besides my income is such that I don't have leftover monthly sums for extras— well, finally, he believed me."

I replaced the daiquiri pitcher in the refrigerator, brought back the gimlet pitcher along with Antoinette's drink. "But you did take the course. How did that happen?"

"Oh, my, yes. Finished it in six months, too, it takes some people years to do all the assignments. That's why I'm here, you see. I'm what Mr. Fenster calls 'living proof' of the advantages of the College of Creative Writing. But I couldn't have managed it if it weren't for Mr. Pendleton. That's why I was so surprised when I found out the—well, I think shoddy is the word—the shoddy way he was running the school. Not at all the sort of thing I expected from one of his stature."

"What did Pendleton do to help you?"

"Mr. Fenster spoke to him and he permitted me, as a very special case, I have a letter signed by him that makes that very clear, to take the course at half price. It just so happened that I had a little nest egg, five hundred dollars in the bank. Great-aunt Reba left it to me, you remember Great-aunt Reba, Brenda? She lived to be a hundred and two? Well, she died a little over two years ago and she left me five hundred dollars which I was saving for a rainy day. . . ." She laughed a tinkling laugh and sipped her drink. "So I was all set!"

I knew that Brenda was thinking what I was thinking.

There was almost a smell of the con game about it. "But you did sell poems after you took the course? You got some return out of it, you did earn some money?" She looked so innocent and trusting, a tiny little old lady with tarnished white curls.

She lowered her lashes. They were long, unexpectedly long, she must have been a pretty girl in her youth. "Well, not exactly. Not yet. Although Mr. Fenster says I'm almost ready for *The New Yorker*."

"But this *Ponder* Magazine you mentioned. Didn't they pay you?"

"No. No, they didn't, but I didn't expect them to. You see, the important thing to do at first is to get printed, to get your name known. *Ponder* is printed by a charity organization, one of these new sensitivity groups, you see, and they need all the money they have for their good works."

Brenda cut in. "Antoinette." She reached for her hand. "How did you get down here? This trip must be rather expensive. The Tiverton House—aren't their rates rather high?"

"You share the room and it isn't so bad, just for two days. I have a roommate, Emily Inch. Perhaps you saw her down at the station, she wears her hair in the modern way, long and straight. Unusual for her age, perhaps, but then she writes plays and you can do just about as you please in the theatre. And the banquet ticket, that was ten dollars which seems terribly extravagant, I know, but

I saved enough for all that. The only problem was transportation, so . . ." She looked defiant. "I hitched a ride!"

"You hitchhiked?" I could see it now. Queen Victoria
on the turnpike, thumbs up.

"No, not hitchhiked. Hitched. I asked around town
until I heard about someone coming to Boston and I asked
if I could come along. Harley Pinkham brought me. He's a
sales representative for an electronics company, he often
comes to Boston, drives all over New England."

"I remember Harley." Brenda smiled. "He's the one
who looks like Pa Kettle."

"Well, yes, he does, now that you mention it. . . ."

The telephone pealed and I answered it. It was my
partner, Barry Parks, and he sounded apologetic. "Knute,
Captain Granger says he knows it's our day off, but . . ."

"What's up?" I wasn't as disappointed as I might have
been if Cousin Antoinette hadn't been there. Oh, I
thought she was a doll, a little old lady doll that you
wound up and it talked—and talked—and talked, but just
the same I wasn't too disappointed to be called away.

"It's this Pendleton thing. We've got three hundred
and fourteen people to talk to in the next twenty-four
hours and Captain Granger figures it's going to take all
of us. And Doc Albert has brought in some preliminary
reports that he wants us all to hear so we'll be filled
in. . . ."

"Okay. Tell him thirty minutes." Time for my share
of the shrimp salad if I gulped it. I told my wife I had to

go out for a while and Brenda gave me a funny look, but Antoinette seemed to think it was just part of the cops and robbers game and asked no questions.

She was doing a play-by-play description of her running battle with the postmistress of her home town who was, it seemed, inordinately nosy, when I ate and ran. Like Mein, I was ready to prowl.

"I couldn't believe my senses." Doc Albert shook his bald head, the overhead light made it gleam like ivory. "I don't think I've come across it in maybe thirty years. In the prepenicillin days it was commonly used for the disease, of course . . . not always effective, too many ifs, ands or buts about it. . . ."

I stared at the Xeroxed sheet they'd handed us. Arsphenamina (arsphen) arsphenamine, U.S.P. (Arsenobenzol, Diarsenol, Salvarsan, diaminodihydroxyarsenobenzene di-hydrochloride) with a lot of chemical symbols trailing after. It contained, according to the single-spaced printing, not less than 30 per cent of arsenic and was . . . I really raised my eyebrows—"a specific remedy for syphilis in all stages."

"You mean this arsphenamine—" I stumbled over the pronunciation—"killed Pendleton? You mean he had a venereal disease?"

Doc Albert shook his head again. "That's just it. It doesn't appear that he did. I'm having some final tests run, but there's no indication at all, I'll bet my bottom dollar he didn't. Yet arsphenamine was in that hypodermic and arsphenamine was injected into his arm. Now"—he stabbed the sheet with his finger—"read that."

I read.

"Arsphenamine sometimes produces toxic results which are similar to poisoning by arsenic. These occur especially after intramuscular injections. Intramuscular injection is painful and is usually followed by a tender, inflammatory nodule, which persists for some time."

I looked up. "Did you have the nodule?"

"He did."

"Where'd this information come from?" I tapped the sheet.

"A 1936 edition of *Useful Drugs*."

I read on.

"For intravenous injection a clear alkaline solution is used. The contents of the tube should be used at once after opening and under no conditions should the contents of a tube damaged in transportation or any remnant of the powder from previously opened tubes be employed."

"Sounds damn dangerous," I said aloud. The next paragraph was ominously headed ACCIDENTS. "A rather common untoward result following intravenous injection is the so-called nitritoid crisis which consists of flushing of the face, rapid flush and dyspnea. Nausea and vomiting and precordial pain may be present; even syncope may occur."

"What," I asked, "is syncope?"

"A partial or complete temporary suspension of respiration and circulation due to cerebral anemia," Dr. Albert answered automatically.

"To put it in my language, a dead duck," I said. "Why would a guy do a chancy thing like injecting himself with that stuff especially if he didn't have the disease to begin with?"

"That," said Doc Albert, eyes gleaming behind his glasses, "is the interesting question. Especially since he ignored one vital precaution. The next paragraph."

I read, "Caution—prior to injection, the solution must be alkalinized with 0.85 cc of normal solution of sodium hydroxide." I looked up. "No sodium hydroxide?"

"Nope. By intent or stupidity." He shrugged.

Parks blushed as he generally did before speaking up in a crowd. "Maybe Pendleton was a hypochondriac."

I agreed with him. "It's got to be something like that. Bugged on pills and medicines, got hold of some he shouldn't have and—lights out."

Captain Granger, sitting silently behind his desk, made a pyramid of his hands. "It would be helpful if one of these people could confirm that."

"When does the mass interrogation begin?" I wanted to know.

"We've got it lined up for the banquet room of the

Tiverton House," Pinky told me. "The Captain's got a corps of stenos coming in, we'll take their statements on the spot. Just the basics, name, address, where were you all day, did you see Pendleton? With a little luck and a lot of hard work, we'll get it done by nighttime."

The door opened behind us and Davoren stuck his head in. "Captain, there's a phone call you'd better take."

"Who is it?"

"She says she's Mrs. Arthur Glenn Pendleton and she says and I quote, where the hell is my husband's body?"

Pinkerton looked stunned. "But—Pomfret said Pendleton hadn't any relatives, no family at all."

I thought back. "They're divorced. Couple of years ago, maybe longer. There was a big stink about it in the papers at the time. What the devil's her name? Zorina, something like that. She accused him of cohabiting with young girls and he countered with something just as sordid, lesbianism or nymphomania, I don't remember."

Granger sighed, picked up his phone, said into it, "This is Captain Granger, ma'am. What can I do for you?"

I could hear her strident answer clear across the captain's desk. "I'll sue you, you know that? You've got no right to cut up my husband's body, not without permission you don't. I can sic the Civil Liberties watchdogs on you . . ."

"You claim to be Mrs. Pendleton, but we have been told that Mr. Pendleton had no family. Aren't you divorced?"

24

"Divorce! Pah! Means no more than the marriage rigamarol. Once mated, always mated. I want Arthur's body and I want it now, you hear!"

"Where do you live, Mrs.—ah—Pendleton?" Granger was frowning, his usually patient tone was gone.

"I? I live in Plymouth. But right now I'm at the Essex Hotel where the bus stops. Just got off the Plymouth-Brockton bus and you can jolly well send a police car over to get me. I'm not spending any money on taxis. . . ."

Davoren was at the door again, making gestures. I went over to see what he wanted this time. "There's a young woman out here," he whispered. "She says Pendleton was her fiancé and she wants to take care of the funeral arrangements."

I looked back at Granger who was attempting to mollify the former Mrs. Pendleton. Pinkerton and Dracut were watching him while Parks and Blaisdell were concentrating on Davoren and me. A two-ring circus. I motioned to Parks to follow and we went out into the squad room to talk to Miss June Carr, aged twenty-two, a breath-taking blonde with lots of curves, and dimpled. A writer, she told us in breathy tones, of Gothic novels.

She carried in one hand a small package of facial tissues and as she sat at my desk, looking as helpless as I'd ever seen a female look, she extracted one of the tissues, dabbed at her big blue eyes and set her lips to quivering. "We were going to be married next month," she gasped

25

and burst into tears. Her top teeth protruded slightly. I wondered fleetingly what it was about buck-teethed girls that made them seem sexy.

Parks got up and got her a cup of water. I simply sat and waited. She fluttered damp eyelashes at Parks when he brought the water, breathed, "Thank you," and tasted it, set it down on my desk. She let the Kleenex drop and took another. Finally, she seemed ready and I asked her if she'd seen Pendleton that morning.

"No, I talked to him on the phone. He was in his room, he wasn't feeling well, he told me." She bravely held back a sob. "I should have gone to him right then and there but I was on a panel."

"A panel?"

"Yes, with Lilly O'Hare, she writes Gothic novels, too, and Mr. Reasoner, he's a paperback editor." The tears resumed, quietly trickled, just enough, quite artistic. "We got so interested, we ran over into lunchtime, so I grabbed a sandwich at the coffee shop and then, instead of going to Arthur, I went to a copyright meeting. Oh," she wailed, "I'll never forgive myself!"

Pinkerton and Dracut came out of the captain's office and went out into the hall. I could tell by their expressions they were on their way to pick up the ex-Mrs. Pendleton. They looked disgusted.

Miss Carr used her tissue with enthusiasm and managed to knock the cup of water off my desk as she did so. Parks went to get her another. When she'd calmed herself again, I asked her if Pendleton was the type of man who was overconcerned about his health.

"Arthur?" She opened her blue eyes even wider. "Why, Arthur was the healthiest man you ever saw! He truly believed in physical fitness, exercises, sports. He had muscles like a—like a boy!"

"Did he seem depressed when you'd been with him lately?"

"Well, I haven't seen him for two weeks, no, I guess it's about three. I live in California, you see, Riverside, but my mother lives in Connecticut and she thought as long as I was coming to this convention, I should take some extra time and visit her. So I did. I mean, I felt I owed it to her and besides, I wanted her to get used to the idea of Arthur. He was older, you see, and . . . we were going to spend a few days with her when this meeting was over!" Here came the tears again.

"That's why you didn't fly in with Pendleton, then." I was halfway talking to myself.

"Oh, I never should have left him!"

By now I guessed the floor around my desk must be littered with Kleenex, she was almost down to the end of her pack. Parks was watching her like a sympathetic mother hen. Hardhearted as I was, I couldn't much blame him. She was a pretty little thing and seemed genuinely upset.

"What did Arthur die of?" she asked piteously. "Nobody told me."

I looked at Parks who blushed and told her, "I guess you could call it a dose of old medicine. A bad reaction."

"Old medicine? You mean he . . . that's why you were asking me about his health. But, whyever . . . whatever for? What kind of medicine was it?"

"Arsphenamine," I answered.

She blinked. I wondered if she was nearsighted. "What on earth is that?"

"It's an out-of-date treatment for venereal disease."

Her pretty pink mouth fell open. Yes, she did have buck teeth. "For what?"

I repeated my sentence, or started to, but she stopped me with waving hands. "You—you must be crazy! Why, Arthur didn't . . . Arthur wouldn't . . . That's the most terrible thing I've ever heard. How can you say such a thing about a man who can't even defend himself? How can you? Dirty minds, that's it. Policemen with dirty minds!"

I tried to tell her, "We didn't say he had . . ." But she wouldn't listen. She jumped to her feet, knocked over the remainder of the second water cup, cried, "I'll get a lawyer. There must be something that can be done about this. Defamation of character, something . . ."

The voice from the hall was louder than hers, much louder, and the sound of it obliterated whatever June Carr had been saying. "I'm cremating Pendleton's body tomorrow, you hear me, and I don't give a damn whether you like it or not. We always agreed we'd be cremated, soon as possible. I've got the agreement we signed right here in my handbag!" And Pinky and Dracut, preceded by a giant of a woman wearing a fantastic full-length peasant-style dress, filled the squad room entrance. Davoren stared open-mouthed.

"Who," breathed June Carr, nostrils pinched, "is that?"

"That's the ex-Mrs. Pendleton." I watched her expression.

Something clicked behind the luminous blue eyes. June clutched her handbag and tissue package close to her agreeable chest, put up her small chin and moved forward just in time to cut off the passage of the trio headed for Captain Granger's office.

"You can't have him," said June Carr in a high, tight voice. "Arthur is going to be buried next to my father in Connecticut."

The female giant—six feet, I guessed, maybe 250 pounds, not fat, just big, turned like an ocean liner with Pinkerton and Dracut in her wake. "Who the hell are you?"

"I'm Junie Carr. Arthur's fiancée." She stood her ground, I had to give her credit for that.

"Arthur's—what?" Majorie Main, in the movies. Earlier Brenda had mentioned Pa Kettle (Percy Kilbride), and now here was Ma Kettle to fill out the cast.

"We were going to be married next month." A slight quivering of Junie's lips.

29

The ex-Mrs. Pendleton's green-grape eyes looked Junie up and down. Then she opened her wide mouth and began to laugh. Her laugh was outsize like the rest of her. She went on and on, laughing. Junie Carr seemed to crumble.

When she'd abruptly stopped laughing, the big woman closed her mouth with a snap, turned, said, "Take me to this Captain Granger," and flanked by her escorts, stamped off.

I told Brenda and Antoinette all about it when I got home.

"My goodness, imagine!" Antoinette seemed fascinated. "What did Junie do then?"

"What else?" I asked. "Began to cry."

"What will they do with his body?"

"That's Granger's problem, not mine. All I'm in for is the mass questioning tomorrow." I pushed Mein down off my lap. "Beat it, cat. I'm going to have a beer and go to bed. Unless"—I turned to Cousin Antoinette—"you want me to take you back to the hotel."

"Oh, I've asked her to stay with us." I thought that Brenda avoided my eyes. "She may have to stay on for several days until this thing is cleared up and there's no need for her to pay a hotel bill when we have a guest room . . ."

I started for the kitchen. "Why not?" It was a thoughtful thing to do. We did have a guest room, even though it was a small room right next to ours and the walls were kind of thin. . . . I'd be childish, indeed, if I minded giving bed and board to a nice little old lady for a couple of days, Brenda's cousin at that . . . only, as I put my hand in the refrigerator to pull out a beer, I realized that I did mind.

I resented it like hell.

After all, we'd only been married for three weeks. We hardly knew each other.

I didn't sleep very well. I'd been right about the thin walls, it seemed I'd heard every move Cousin Antoinette made during the night, so I was on the grumpy side when we began to run through the routine at the Tiverton House the next morning.

Parks and I had one Derek Pomfret for starters.

Derek Pomfret was the one with the beard, all right. His strange-colored eyes, they were closer to yellow than green, made me think somehow of jungles. He was polite, no, more than that—anxious to help. Pendleton had been, he began by saying, a good employer.

"How long have you worked for him?"

"Almost six months. I was studying for my master's at UCLA. He made me such a good offer, I thought my master's could wait for a bit. Besides, my field is the twentieth-century novel. He was a living source."

"You knew about his engagement to Miss Carr?"

Pomfret studied his fingernails. "Yes—and no."

I glanced at him sharply. "What does that mean?"

"I knew he'd been seeing her until she came East. I

31

knew he got letters from her marked personal that he presumably answered himself. But he hadn't confided his plans to me. I could only assume he was interested in the young lady, but interested enough to marry her?" He looked thoughtful. "To tell you the truth, and this is merely an opinion, he didn't behave like a man who planned to be married. But I suppose we'll have to take Miss Carr's word for it."

"What motive would she have for lying?"

"Maybe she believes it. Maybe it was so. I don't know. I really don't know, I shouldn't surmise—only, the publicity might further her career, you know. Perhaps she isn't an opportunist, I may be doing her an injustice. At any rate, it doesn't matter any more, does it?" He didn't expect an answer to his rhetorical question, so I didn't give him the one I had ready—that, yes, it did matter. At least might matter.

Parks spoke up. "Did he have many women friends?"

Pomfret shrugged. "He had a lot of female attention, if that's what you mean. If he spoke at a college, he was picked at and confronted by the girls. That's an indication these days that they liked him. And when he spoke to a woman's club . . ." He rolled his eyes ceilingward. "They went ape. It irritated Penn, but he liked it, too."

"Did he go out with any of them—other than Miss Carr?" I could guess at Parks' train of thought—if Pendleton suspected that he had VD, he'd have to suspect that he got it somewhere.

"Every so often. Miss Carr was the only steady one during my tenure."

I was interested in the trip from California. "You said your plane arrived at about eleven—you must have left the West coast pretty early?" Too early, in fact, was my hunch. Four hours' difference plus at least three hours' flying time. That would set their departure at around four in the morning. I didn't think planes left at that early hour. Maybe they did, but I didn't think so.

"Oh, we didn't come from California." Pomfret looked surprised at the very idea. "We came in from Kansas City."

"Kansas City?"

"Yes, Penn's home was near there—a little town called Liberal, Kansas. He wrote about it in *Backward, Turn Backward*. He felt sentimental about the place, stopped when he got a chance and visited his father's grave, that's what he told me. Anyway, he had me set up a stopover there, so I did."

"Did he visit with anyone there?" I leaned forward. Somebody from the past, just the ticket. Just the place, maybe, to pick up some do-it-yourself medicine from an old friend. A discreet old friend.

Pomfret shook his head. "It was rather sad, really. We hired a car and drove out of the city to Liberal. He had me take him by the house he lived in, it's one of those ghastly old boardinghouses now, and then he told me various streets to turn down and go slow, but we never

33

stopped anywhere. Not until we got to the cemetery. That was pretty forlorn, too, except for the Pendleton plot. Nice big headstone, expensive one as well. Carefully kept with urns of geraniums around. He got out and looked at it for a few minutes, then he got back in the car. As we drove out of the cemetery, he said, 'That's where I want to be planted, Derek, my boy. Don't you forget that.'" Pomfret dropped his eyelids to hide whatever expression was there.

"He was morose, then?" Now we were getting on with it. Suicide in mind? Maybe. If he thought he had an unbearable disease. But why the routine with that out-of-date medicine? That part didn't fit in the picture I was painting in my mind, not at all.

Pomfret looked directly at me. "I wouldn't say morose. More like a man who'd made a decision." He paused. "Yes, now that I think of it. As though he'd been toying with an idea, made up his mind and had no more doubts. After that, we went bowling. He seemed to enjoy himself. 'Couple of boys on a men's night out,' he told me. Got up the next morning, caught an early plane, or I should say a plane that was supposed to be early, but wasn't. Equipment failure, the airline people called it, sent for another ship. Anyway, finally we took off and landed here. And he was air sick."

"Was that usual?"

"Maybe every other flight or so. He hated flying, but he made himself do it. Said it was the only sensible way to travel and he'd be damned if he'd let his bloody stomach turn him off. He was like that."

"Let's get back to this decision business. In view of what happened here, could he have been contemplating suicide? Decided then and there to go ahead with it?"

He stared at me, no, in my direction. I wasn't sure what he was looking at. "I refuse to feel guilty," he said suddenly. "I wasn't his keeper, he was a grown man, successful, moody. I wasn't paid to read his complicated mind. And besides, how could I have guessed such a thing? Just because he wanted to visit his father's grave? Lots of people visit graves without killing themselves!"

His tone had grown louder, more insistent. The idea hurt him, I thought. The possibility that, with understanding, he might have been his brother's keeper after all. And then, I couldn't help it, I stifled a yawn. I was tired. I watched his face close completely and I asked, "Who did he talk to when he got to Boston?"

Pomfret shrugged. "Nobody."

"You mean he saw no one he knew—no one at all?"

"That's what I said, isn't it? We came directly to the hotel from the airport. . . ."

"How?"

"By taxi, of course."

"Then he talked to the cab driver."

Pomfret made an impatient sound. "Well, of course, if you mean . . . we sat in the back, the driver sat in the front. They didn't communicate at all. Except," and now he was becoming sarcastic, "that Penn said Hotel Tiverton, please. Or something like that."

"All right." I waved him to silence. "Then what?"

"We came in and registered. Yes, he did say something to the room clerk, good morning or some such, and heaven knows which room clerk because I don't remember what he looked like. And there was the bellboy who brought his bags up, but again I don't think I could tell you which one. We came in the room, he went into his bedroom, the bellboy pushed light switches, the usual things, took my tip and left. Penn went right to bed and stayed there. The only person who came into the room other than myself and the bellboy was Miss Evers. At least while I was there."

I said to Parks, "Then he must have brought the arsphenamine with him."

Pomfret disagreed vehemently. "But I assure you, he didn't. I packed the suitcases myself. I locked them and kept the keys. There was no hypodermic needle nor any other medicine in either bag. Not even aspirin. Penn didn't believe in it."

"What do you mean, he didn't believe in it?"

"He was anti-anything that smacked of drugs. He used to say he would have made a good Christian Scientist."

I stared at the bearded secretary. "Now, let's be certain about this—he didn't bring the arsphenamine with him, he didn't get it en route and he didn't see anyone here who could have given it to him?"

36

Pomfret nodded in positive agreement. "That's it."

"On his person? Could he have carried it on his person?"

Pomfret fiddled with his beard. "I can't say for certain, of course, but I seriously doubt it. I act as a quasi valet, I put his suit out, I don't remember doing it specifically but I generally check the pockets—and the suit he wore came right from the cleaner's bag, I remember that."

I leaned on my elbows, stared at him. "But, man, he had to get it from somewhere. It was there."

The yellow eyes stared back at me unblinkingly. "I know. But I don't have the answer."

"Did you go into his bedroom at the Tiverton?" Parks wanted to know.

Pomfret's head twisted so he could look at Parks. "No, I don't think I did. The bellboy took his bag in—or did Penn take it from him at the door?" He shook his head. "I can't remember. Anyway, he went right in and shut the door. He felt lousy."

"Then the arsphenamine and the hypodermic could have been there," said Parks to me. "Waiting for him."

I thought about it. "I suppose it could have been. But how the devil did somebody get him to use it?"

"Never in a million years," said Pomfret with authority. "I told you—it was utterly and totally against his principles."

Maybe, I thought. Yes, maybe. Only how do you know

37

what you'd do if you were ill, or thought you were ill, and desperate?

"What was the stuff, anyway?" Pomfret asked me. "Nobody's said."

I told him.

He said, "You're kidding. You've got to be kidding. Not Arthur Glenn Pendleton." He was incredulous. It was as though I'd suggested the Pope had a concubine.

"He didn't have VD," I told him. "The doctor's verified that."

"Oh, my God." Pomfret looked horrified. "What if he thought he had it . . . If I thought I did, I'd . . . oh, my God." His golden eyes tarnished.

"It can be cured," I told him.

Pomfret shuddered elaborately and Parks pulled a paper out of his coat pocket, passed a pamphlet over to me. "I asked Doc Albert to give me something on it," he explained.

The pamphlet was headed "Venereal Disease" and was written by a Dr. Fiumara of the Division of Communicable Diseases, Massachusetts Department of Public Health.

"I'll look at it," I promised and stuck it in my own pocket. Concentrating on the secretary, I said, "Assuming that for some reason he thought he had syphilis, the question remains—how and where did he get the arsphenamine? Why didn't he go to a doctor for the proper treatment . . . ?"

"I can only guess. He didn't like doctors. I should have put that in stronger terms—he had an aversion to those in the medical profession that bordered on mania. Let me give you an example. Shortly after I entered his employ, his tax accountant suggested he take out a very large insurance policy. Naturally, it involved a doctor's examination. He balked. Absolutely balked. And he told me that he carried no insurance at all—none. Remarkable thing for a man in his position. His comment was, if I remember correctly, 'I'll be damned if I'll let those murdering quacks lay as much as a finger on my pulse.'"

"Can we make another guess—that he might have gone to a friend for advice? It seems to me he would have had to ask someone."

Pomfret shuddered again, thought about my question. "I would think he would be more likely to read up on it, try to treat it on his own."

"But where did he get the arsphenamine? You don't just walk into any drugstore and pick it up from the counter." I wondered aloud, "Has anybody checked the Tiverton House pharmacy?"

"He didn't get it there," Parks replied. "Pinkerton said they checked the pharmacy right off."

"Gentlemen," Pomfret still looked shaken, "I just can't help you on that." He pushed his cuff back, looked at his watch. "I'm due at the airport shortly, Penn's publisher is flying up from New York and I'm to meet him."

"And his publisher is . . . ?"

"Stacy Dellevand. He's worked with Penn for years. He'd be able to tell you more than I, I should think. They were pretty close. As close as Penn was with anyone so far as I knew."

"Tell him we'd like to see him. Bring him around when he gets here."

"I'll try."

"What do you mean—try?"

"I don't mean anything. I'll tell him, that's all I mean." It seemed to me that Pomfret was getting edgy, but I had another question.

"What about a will?"

"I suppose he had one. A man in his position."

"You don't know?"

"The subject never came up. He's got a lawyer in New York who handles his affairs. I never thought to notify him—perhaps Dellevand did."

"What's the lawyer's name?"

"Klineman. Harold Klineman. The address and phone number's in his address book in the suite. I'd better call him right away."

"Yes, you'd better. We want to communicate with him, too." Pomfret wasn't operating too efficiently, I reflected, but that was natural enough under the circumstances. "Okay," I told him. "Thanks. If we need anything more from you personally, we'll let you know." I penned a memo in the margin of my notebook. Stacy Dellevand and Harold Klineman. Pomfret, leaving, verified the spelling. I added—maybe get blood checks on June Carr and the ex-Mrs. Pendleton. Zelinda Pendleton, that was her name. After that reminder, I wrote 'and others?'. What others? If Pendleton wasn't ill, how did he get the idea that he was? There had to have been a logical source.

G. Harding Fenster was our next interviewee. The executive director of the writing school was a slender, dapper man, aged about fifty, I estimated. His shirt was the whitest of whites, his blue suit perfectly pressed, his necktie neatly striped in muted tones of blue. It was evident that his mind was on the future of the school because the first thing he said when he sat down was "I protest this harassment. For the life of me, I cannot see why you must bedevil three hundred persons, most of whom never laid eyes on Arthur Glenn Pendleton."

"The man is dead," I reminded him coldly. "Dead under strange circumstances. What would you have us do? Say, too bad, but none of you could have had anything to do with it, so go home?"

He gnawed at his long upper lip. "It seems completely obvious to me that the man committed suicide. I've been told about the purpose of the drug involved. How could any of these people be held responsible?"

"We don't know that he committed suicide at all, but if he did, it is possible that he was goaded—or even pushed into it. Did he ever talk to you about his health?"

Fenster extracted a cigarette, lit it. "Mr. Pendleton and I did not often see one another."

"But he was the head of your school?"

Fenster held his cigarette out and looked at the shape of it. "In name only. Titular. I ran—run the College of Creative Writing. And I intend to continue, unless, of course, this ugly publicity blows things sky high."

"There's been nothing in the papers about the VD angle."

"So far." He spoke bitterly.

I knew better than to promise there wouldn't be. Word has a way of getting around, particularly a word like syphilis with all its sensational connotations.

"How much income did Mr. Pendleton derive from the school?" Parks asked him.

Fenster came close to sneering. "For the use of his name, you mean? Far more than he should have."

I was curious too. "How much?"

His face smoothed, eyes hooded ever so slightly. "It depended on the enrollment, of course. He received a percentage. In a good year, I'd say . . ." He hesitated. "It's only a guess, I'd have to look at the books. Maybe—thirty thousand?"

I whistled softly. "Not bad for the use of a name." I did some mental arithmetic. Three hundred and eight at one thousand dollars—no, Antoinette had said there were over six hundred students—six hundred thousand dollars! That was a lot of nice cabbage, indeed. If Pendleton got, say, 10 per cent of the gross, it would have been more like sixty thousand than thirty thousand. Enough to want him out of the profit picture, I wondered. Could be, could well be.

"What will you do now that he's gone?" Parks was still pursuing his subject. "Get another big name writer?"

Fenster's face was inscrutable. "Possibly. It may not be necessary. I have my staff. They are the people who do all the real work."

"And you say Pendleton never did anything?" I asked. "Never looked over a manuscript, sold an enrollment?"

"He did discuss the school at group meetings." Fenster seemed loath to give him that much credit.

"And he did come here in person, to this shindig," I pointed out.

"Yes. He provided a certain amount of window dressing." The unspoken implication was but not thirty—or forty—or fifty or whatever it was—dollars' worth.

"How long have you known Pendleton?" was my next question.

"The school has been in operation six years," Fenster said stiffly.

"Who hired whom?"

He blinked like a lizard. "I beg your pardon?"

"Did you tie Pendleton into the school or did he bring you in?"

Even more stiffly, "He contacted me. He had some crude idea about cashing in on something like the Famous

Writers School, but he hadn't any idea at all how to go about it. I'd written, taught writing, acted as an agent all my adult life. I brought the College into being."

"Then you knew his former wife?" asked Parks.

"Zelinda." Fenster permitted himself a small, tight smile. "Anyone within shouting distance knew Zelinda."

"What caused their split-up?" I wanted to know.

A supercilious raising of the eyebrows. "Have you met the lady?"

"I've seen her."

"Need I answer?"

I thought, but didn't say, one man's meat . . . "Were you told that he intended to marry Miss Carr?"

The eyebrows jumped, this time from sheer surprise. Then, "I told you, Pendleton and I were not intimates. We were not apt to exchange that sort of information."

"Did you see him or talk to him at all yesterday?" My final question, Fenster obviously didn't give a damn about what happened to Pendleton, there wasn't much point in digging further without any sort of crowbar.

"I did not. I was told he arrived just before noon. At the time, I was closeted with the functions manager of the hotel, going over final arrangements for the banquet that was to be held tonight." He scowled. "They'll keep the deposit, of course. Even though under the circumstances, one would think . . ." He didn't finish his sentence. Functions managers were clearly beneath his contempt.

I remembered something. "I thought Pomfret had to go

down to the banquet hall to take care of arrangements? Later. So that he left Pendleton alone."

Fenster looked at me coldly. "I knew nothing about it. It was all arranged before noon."

"Oh?" I exchanged glances with Parks. Another session with Derek Pomfret seemed to be in order. And one with the functions manager, too.

"Is that all? Are you through with me? I would like to be free to attempt, at least, to placate my students. They aren't accustomed to this sort of treatment . . ."

"Miss Antoinette Evers," I cut in. "You accepted her at half tuition. Why?"

"Who?" He was part way out of his chair. "Oh, yes, Miss Evers. Because that was all she could afford. She pleaded with me and—I'm not a heartless man. Although you obviously think I am."

"And Arthur Pendleton had nothing to do with it?"

"Oh, he had to get in on the act, that was the way he was. He wrote her some noblesse oblige letter. But it was my idea even though he did his best to take credit for it." He stood erect. "There's nothing more I can tell you."

I watched him for a moment, then sat back and let him go. "Parks," I said thoughtfully, "what about these phone calls? Can't the switchboard give us some data on who called Pendleton—or whom he called?"

"Pinky checked that out. It's in his report, maybe you didn't see it. The hotel's got a complex board, lots of automatic stuff. Several operators, too. The suite had two separate phones—it's suite 2660–2661. Pomfret had the 2660 number and Pendleton had 2661. The only thing Pinkerton could come up with was that the information operator remembered that some woman called asking for Pendleton's number. That could be Miss Evers, when she called and asked to see him."

I sighed. "That figures. Better do it the hard way, then. Be sure somebody checks out Pomfret's alleged whereabouts after he left the suite."

Parks nodded and went out, bearing the message about the functions manager. When he returned, he brought a male peacock with him. Slouch hat, shades of the late John Barrymore, brocade vest with matching tie and over-the-ankle, pearl-buttoned boots yet. Its name was Clancy Hettrick.

We went through the preliminaries in good order. Then he leaned back, draped an arm over the chair back, and said, "You realize, of course, this should be only the beginning?"

I took my bemused attention off his high-button shoes and asked, "What?"

"Only the beginning. Chapter one. Dead body. By Chapter five or six there should be another. At least. And one big gory one for the end." He smiled affably. His teeth hardly showed when he smiled. I was reminded of Bela Lugosi as Count Dracula.

"What do you write, Mr. Hettrick?"

"Murder mysteries. Couldn't you tell?"

"Do you sell them?"

"Haven't yet, old boy. But I've got a goodie going the paperback rounds now. Lots of sex. And six—count 'em —bloody corpses." Again the smile.

I bit back an answer, got down to business. "You arrived at the Tiverton House when?"

"The night before. Had to, couldn't get a flight otherwise. All booked up." He'd flown in from Cleveland at 6 P.M., he told me. "Made myself known to the staff, they were there already. Had never met any of them before. Corresponded with Miss Quigley, got chummy with her right off. Spent the whole evening in Annie's company. Charming woman. Ugly as hell, but so pizzazz."

Lucky Annie, I thought. "Did you see Pendleton when he arrived yesterday morning?"

"Never laid eyes on him. Sacked in late. Carousing, you know." He winked.

"Your room was on the fifteenth floor?"

"Right. Next to Junie. Didn't know that till later on or I might have bypassed Annie. Junie's a dish. Have you seen her?"

"Miss Carr? Yes, we've talked to her." I couldn't resist adding, "She says she was going to marry Pendleton."

"Little Junie?" He pulled a face. "Pendleton was a lecher."

"I thought you said you'd never seen him."

47

"That's because I haven't, old boy. But I read, you know." He shook his slouch-hatted head. "He must have really pulled the wool over her young eyes."

"Read? Read what? Where did you read that Pendleton was a lecher?"

"His books, old boy. Takes the mind of a dirty old man to write that bilge." The seemingly toothless smile came, went. "Don't tell me you haven't read them?"

I regarded him thoughtfully. "Perhaps I should."

Hettrick snickered. "When you've got nothing better to do."

"A saint. The man was a saint." Eva Lynn Lamb was her name and she was the middle-aged, hard-eyed, pinched-mouth woman I'd spotted in the squad room yesterday.

"How well did you know Pendleton, Mrs. Lamb?"

"Miss Lamb. I've known Arthur—Mr. Pendleton for years. He once bought a beagle puppy from my kennel. I raise dogs, you see, write about them, too. Arthur—Mr. Pendleton was devoted to animals. Especially dogs. He was brokenhearted when the little bitch I sold him was killed by a car."

So she raised dogs in—I checked the home address— Scottsdale, Arizona. Long way to go from California for a dog, I thought, but then I was a cat man myself. I looked into her close-set eyes and wondered what kind of a kennel

48

mistress she made. One thing for certain, I needn't ask if she'd been romantically involved with Arthur Pendleton. But, to my surprise, Parks asked her.

"Were you—ah—personally fond of Mr. Pendleton?"

I expected her to snap at that, but instead she nearly simpered. "Dear me, no. I mean, one didn't think of him in that way. He was above such things, even though some women did have a tendency to think otherwise. But I will say, we were very good friends." Her mouth closed smugly on the word friends.

"Some women?" I picked up her remark.

"He spent some time at a ranch in my part of the world one summer." She giggled, actually giggled. "You should have seen those summer people. Women from the East with their hair all lacquered on top of their heads. Swarmed like bees. He was kind to them, polite, but—he used to come to see me and he'd say, 'Eva Lynn, they are poor carnal creatures.'"

"What was he doing at the ranch?"

"Vacationing. He loved riding. Horses, you know. A real man's man. And he did some hunting. Rabbits, especially. He was an excellent shot."

"I thought you said he was an animal lover?"

"Oh, he was," she assured me. "But jack rabbits are a terrible problem out our way. He was conservation minded, you see. Control the rabbit population and you have a better life for the rabbits."

We'd gone far afield, I could hardly see how Pendle-

49

ton's attitude toward rabbits had any bearing on his death. But the gun business—if he were such a good shot and bent on suicide, wouldn't he have shot himself instead? I didn't waste time wondering about it, I'd given up on the idea of suicide. More than likely the whole business was accidental. He got hold of some dated drug to cure what he thought was a disease and the medicine killed him. That's the way it looked to me and I wondered if we'd ever find out where he got the stuff. We determined that Miss Lamb hadn't seen him here before his death and let her go. We had still a half-dozen people to question before noon including Emily Inch, Antoinette's roommate and lady playwright.

"I've been making some notes . . . this terrible tragedy has so many dramatic overtones, and everything is grist for the writer's mill." She pushed at her long hair unconsciously and waited eagerly, pad in hand. No doubt her next three-act would include a police interview scene.

No, she hadn't known Arthur Glenn Pendleton personally, but she found him "most interesting. One of the last of the giants. I can't tell you how marvelous it is to be here . . . if it had to happen, I mean. Being on the scene, you see, I can do such an authentic version. I'm so anxious to get to work before someone else steals my idea. I plan to call it *The Life and Death of Arthur Glenn Pendleton* . . . a long title, but what about *Marat/Sade?*" She literally squirmed with excitement.

Parks had a question for her. "Miss Evers shared a

room with you. Did she say anything about going to see
Mr. Pendleton?"

"No, no, she didn't. But then we hadn't had a chance
to talk much, I must ask her for all the firsthand details.
How the suite looked and just what was said and done
. . . this will be an absolute triumph. I feel it—in my very
bones!"

I hoped fervently that she wouldn't trace Antoinette to
my apartment and started to ease her out, but Parks wasn't
quite through. "What did you and Miss Evers talk about?"

I didn't stare at him, but I wanted to. Did he have
some bee in his beret about Antoinette? She was in the
sitting room while he died, but where would she have
gotten hold of anything like arsphenamine? And even
more important, what motive could she possibly have
for harming Pendleton?

"Our work, of course," Emily Inch answered. "When
two writers get together, that's all they ever talk about.
She's a poet, but I suppose you know that. Such a
pleasant, sensitive woman. I wish we'd had more time
together, but she's gone to stay with some relative while
this thing gets settled. I shall remain a few days, even if
you fellows tell us we can leave. I can work right here in
the hotel . . . I carry my portable wherever I go, and the
atmosphere is all around me. . . ."

We'd heard the three acts in summary before we got
rid of her and by that time I was starving. We decided that
the coffee shop would be the quickest and went out to tell

Pinkerton we were going, would be back as soon as possible. He and Dracut were talking to Ann Quigley, the assistant that Hettrick had described as ugly but with pizzazz. The first half of his description was correct at any rate, she had lots of straight dark hair that grew low on her forehead and deep circles under great dark eyes. From what I could make of the conversation, she'd seldom seen Pendleton. I thought of a new title for Emily Inch's play: *The Man Nobody Knew.*

When we came back, Dellevand had arrived and Klineman, the lawyer, was with him. The two men, standout VIP types, stood just inside the door to Pinkerton's bailiwick—the hotel had permitted us to utilize unoccupied function rooms—and Pinkerton, looking somewhat flustered, motioned to us to take the new arrivals in tow.

I introduced myself and Parks, led the two men to our temporary "office." Dellevand was a good-looking man with a fine head of wavy silver hair and a ruddy complexion. Klineman was balding, sallow-skinned, on the small side. They both epitomized success.

"Ghastly thing. Ghastly," sighed Dellevand, sitting. "When I got his letter I was thunderstruck—appalled. Bad enough to lose him, but . . ." He shuddered, collected himself sufficiently to hand me a thick envelope. "I brought it with me. Klineman here assured me you'd be discreet." He looked at me anxiously while I wondered what he was talking about. I nodded knowingly, kept a poker face as I opened the envelope and removed several pages of typewritten material.

"You received this when?" I asked Dellevand.

"Yesterday. In the late afternoon mail. I put in an immediate call to California, I wasn't sure where he was. I couldn't reach him, of course, and before I could run him down in Boston, I was notified. . . ." He shook his silvery head solemnly. "What a waste, what a waste."

I devoted my full attention to the letter.

Dear Dell, (I read.)

By the time you read this, I'll be dead.

By my own hand.

I'll leave no note, I don't owe an explanation to anyone except possibly you. If only because you've made it possible for me to die a rich man. Which, in some damned devilish way, has something to do with my dying. But no matter.

You never knew my father, Dell, he died before we ever encountered one another. Died when I was still just a boy, really. Killed himself. You never knew that, did you?

He was a bit of a rounder, my father. Best father a boy ever had. I didn't even miss a mother. He took me everywhere, told me everything. He was my friend, my confidant, my god.

And then one day, he did the worst thing to me he could possibly do. He killed himself.

53

He had syphilis, you see. He didn't tell me that. Went to some two-bit doctor who diagnosed it, gave him some junk to 'cure' it. Cure it! Hell.

I remember his final weeks very well. I wondered what was wrong—he stayed drunk in his room, either wouldn't talk at all or shouted. His eyes sunk into his head, his hands shook, his lips seemed to be shrinking. I can see him yet, pink gums and yellow-white teeth, smiling a smile that was not a smile.

And then one day I came home from high school as usual. It was a hot day, I recall, in summer. The radio was playing—loud. I turned it down and went to his door, called, "Dad?" He didn't answer.

I opened the door. The windows were shut and the shades were drawn. God, it was like an oven! He was lying on the bed. I shot the shade up, said, "Dad" again, leaned over him.

He was dead.

On the table beside the bed was a hypodermic needle with an empty silver-colored tube beside it. The label on the tube read arsphenamine. In the drawer of that table were more of the tubes, a bottle marked sodium hydroxide and a prescription from a Dr. Boine.

I grabbed the prescription with the address on it and I ran all the way to that doctor's office, a dingy little room over an even dingier drugstore. This Dr. Boine was sitting there, eating a sandwich. A slimy little man with a ferret face. He had crumbs on his white jacket.

I waved the prescription in his evil face and I cried, "You killed my father!"

I hit him, he looked so surprised sitting there, mouth part open with a bite of sandwich in it, unchewed.

Then he stood up and belted me one, got me down—I was a skinny kid—and when I gave up, began to cry like a baby, he said, "All right, kid. Who's your father?"

Somehow I told him. I could hardly speak.

"Okay," he said, "let's go look at him. You got a car?"

Weeping, I shook my head. He looked disgusted. "Money for a cab?" he wanted to know.

I had a dollar and some change in my pocket. I gave him the dollar. He yanked me up. "Stop blubbering and come on." But I couldn't stop. I cried all the way home during that ride. The driver kept looking at me in the rear-view mirror. "His old man's sick," Boine told him.

Inside the hot little room, Boine didn't even seem to notice the heat and the smells. Whiskey, vomit, sweat, urine, all mixed up and coming out the odor of suffering.

He leaned over and examined my father. "He's dead all right, kid." Absolutely no emotion. He examined the hypodermic needle, my father's arm. "Damn fool," he muttered.

I stopped crying at that exact moment. Just stopped. Like that. "What do you mean?" I asked him.

"I told him he had to be careful with this stuff." He reached into the half-open drawer, I'd left it that way, and removed the remainder of the tubes, put them in his pocket. "He didn't pay any attention," he went on muttering. "Just drove the stuff in his arm and killed himself."

"Killed himself?" My tongue didn't pronounce the words properly, it wanted to cling to the roof of my mouth.

"Don't worry, it won't say that on the death certificate." He took the sodium hydroxide bottle too. "I'll fix it up for you." He paused, licked his lips with a pointed tongue. "He still owed me for his last visit."

"His last visit? What was wrong with him?"

"He had syphilis. V.D. He owes me five bucks."

I stared at him. I wanted to kill him, to pound him to death with my fists. I swallowed hard. "Write the death certificate. I'll pay you. But don't say anything about—anything."

He nodded, opened the shabby black bag he carried in one hand. "I'll call it neurorecidive resulting in cardiac arrest," he pontificated and when I asked him what that meant, he told me, "Nervous relapse followed by heart failure."

Numbly I watched him fill out a paper. When he held it out in his hand, I noticed that his fingernails were all bitten down. I didn't even want to touch him, I caught the end of the form between my fingertips, but he held on. "The five bucks," he reminded me.

I had to reach in my father's hip pocket to get his wallet. I traded the bill for the death certificate, he must have need for death certificates I thought, he came prepared. "What do I do now?" I wasn't really talking to him.

"Call a neighbor. Call the cops. Call the undertaker. Call anybody you want to. Tell 'em his doctor's come and gone and show 'em that." He closed his bag with a snap. "Damn fool," he said to my father. "I told you you had to alkalinize the arsphenamine in sodium hydroxide."

He started for the door. Every nerve, every muscle in my body had to be controlled to keep me from hurling myself at him. But I didn't. If I did anything to him, he'd tell about my father. And no matter what, nobody must know.

I felt shame, the kind of shame I have never felt before or since but have never forgotten.

So that's how my father died. And that may explain to you my intense hatred of the medical profession. Oh, yes, I know. He was a rare bird, a bad doctor in every sense. I've grown older and matured, but still his face comes back to me every time I even walk by an M.D.'s door.

Which brings me to my own suicide. No wait, there's a middle to this story. From the day they put my father in the ground, I knew that one day I would die the same way. I knew it in a blinding flash and I've never ceased to know it. I think I courted that fate. I bedded down with vile women from time to time, thinking as I did so, now it will come to pass. And when it didn't, then I would hope for a few days at least that my obsession was unfounded, that I had imagined it only because I loved my father so. But eventually, the fear would return and haunt me, haunt me. . . .

And now it has happened. It's almost a relief. I have been told that I have reason to believe I could have this cursed ailment, the scourge of mankind for centuries. Have I gone to a doctor to confirm this possibility? No, I have not. I don't need to. I watched my father and I have his symptoms. I know, you see, I know. Remember the old story about the merchant readying for a trip to Samarkand who was told he would die in Samarkand? And so he ran away, as far as he could from that city, all his life avoided Samarkand until at last in some faraway place he met a man he knew was death and death said, "What are you doing here? I expected to see you in Samarkand?" I have come to Samarkand.

There is one person I can trust to do as I ask, one person who knows my story, all of it, and this person has promised to bring me the arsphenamine.

I shall inject it into my arm just as my father did —without the magic sodium hydroxide—and then all will be made right. All.

No son of mine will watch his father die of syphilis.

Forgive me, Dell, for my sins and omissions. There's a book in California—maybe it's in good enough shape to pay off some of my "debts" to you. Thanks for the buggy ride, it was great while it lasted.

And take some advice, my friend—keep the hell out of Samarkand.

It was signed with big scrawling letters, Arthur Glenn Pendleton. It was dated two days prior to his death and it bore a California airmail postmark.

I handed the letter to Parks without explanation. To Dellevand I said, "So he came to Boston to do this thing? Set it up and went through with it."

"It would seem so."

"Suppose something had gone wrong? Wasn't he taking a chance? Suppose you'd received it before he'd had a chance to follow through?"

Devellevand tapped nervous fingers on the table top. "He must have been pretty sure of the way things would go. Perhaps he even sent it to guarantee he wouldn't change his mind."

Klineman's mouth twisted. "How could he be such a damn fool?" And then, as though he'd realized he'd quoted the nefarious Dr. Boine, he looked abashed.

Dellevand sighed. "You'd have to know Penn. He had certain unshakable attitudes, particularly about such things as manliness, inner courage. The Spartan boy who let the fox eat out his insides was a sissy compared to Penn in some things."

"It's almost as though he weren't quite sane about disease and doctors, his father . . ." Klineman couldn't find words to finish the sentence.

I nodded absent-mindedly. All I could think of was who was the person who could be trusted to do as Pendleton wished? Who had the power to keep that man from killing himself, but didn't? Who—was a murderer in every way but name only?

Klineman cleared his throat. "Detective Pinkerton— was that his name? So apt. Detective Pinkerton said there was some question of place of interment." The lawyer's expression told me he thought any such question in extremely bad taste. "Mr. Pendleton left explicit instructions that he was to be buried alongside his father in Kansas."

So Pomfret had said. Score one for Pomfret. I tried to

visualize Zelinda Pendleton's reaction or that of June Carr. Happily, that was Klineman's problem, not mine. I had bigger—well maybe not bigger—but other fish to fry.

"Now, about the will . . ." I began, but Dellevand interrupted.

"I'm hoping you'll permit Pomfret to fly out of here with me this afternoon. Penn was working on a new book and I'm going to California right away to determine what can be done with it."

"Captain Granger will have to make that decision, Mr. Dellevand. Could you tell me . . . ?"

"Where can I find Captain Granger?" Obviously, Dellevand was used to having things his way.

"Minding the store." I didn't care if it did sound sarcastic.

Dellevand eyed me dispassionately. "And where might that be?"

"Station One. We'll send you over as soon as you've answered some questions." If he could be unflappable, so could I.

When he didn't respond, I took silence for acquiescence and picked up where I'd left off with Klineman. "You say Pendleton left instructions for burial. I presume he also left a will?"

"He did."

"Would you tell me the provisions of that will?"

The little attorney leaned forward. "In view of Pendleton's letter, I assume his death will be ruled a suicide. I don't see how the particulars of his will would have any bearing on the matter."

I hedged. "We are only assuming it was suicide at this point, Mr. Klineman. I suppose," I spoke to Dellevand, "you'd swear the letter was signed by the man?"

"Of course. I'd know his scrawl anywhere and the writing could be no one else's, it's his style, all that emotion, and all that total recall." Dellevand moved impatiently, said to the lawyer, "Tell him what he wants to know, Harold. I've got a plane to catch."

Klineman frowned thoughtfully. "I see. You're interested in the supplier of the drug, is that it? You think the beneficiaries might shed some light?"

I nodded. I was getting as restless as Dellevand.

"There are two. Franklin Edward Clements and Virginia Hanks Clements, husband and wife, of Tarrytown, New York."

"No one else?" I don't know what I expected—somebody who was in Boston when he died? But what did that matter? Whoever put him on to arsphenamine—if someone did—could have been miles away at the time of death. In Tarrytown, New York, for instance.

"Are they relatives?"

"No, not related at all. Arthur had no surviving relatives, at least that's what he assured me. He didn't explain his relationship with the Clementses, said, in fact, it was none of my business. I said, in that case, he'd better be absolutely certain that the names were correct.

He said they were. I said, now you've added the words husband and wife. Suppose this is not their status when the will is executed? And Arthur said, you mean if they're separated? I replied, yes—or if one of them is deceased." The little lawyer, well launched on his subject now, crossed his legs, continued.

"Arthur pondered that for a few minutes and finally he asserted that if the Clementses were divorced, the estate should go to Virginia Hanks Clements. Should either be deceased, the other was to inherit. So then I said, what if both are deceased? Arthur pondered that question much longer."

"I never heard him mention anyone named Clements," Dellevand spoke up. From the slightly sour-grapes expression on his face, I surmised that he was just a little disappointed that he hadn't made the list. "When was this will made, anyway?"

"About eight months ago." Klineman ignored the rest of Dellevand's remark. "After he'd fully considered, Arthur told me to name the Clements' heirs as legatees. Or heir, as the case might be. I, he said, was to be executor and he did add one other clause to this quite simple document. Simple, I say, considering the estate involved."

"And the other clause?" Klineman's verbosity seemed to come in fits and starts. Possibly he, too, was an incipient dramatist.

"Arthur Glenn Pendleton left the sum of one dollar to his former wife, Zelinda Gresham Pendleton."

That amused Dellevand. He laughed out loud.

"How large—roughly—is the estate?"

Klineman pursed his lips. "I should guess—considering copyrights and all—over a million dollars."

Now Dellevand looked definitely depressed.

"Nothing to his secretary? Or to his fiancée?" I was still trying to tie somebody in.

Klineman shook his head and Dellevand snorted. "Who was it this time?" asked the publisher.

"A Miss June Carr. She says they were to be married next month. He hadn't told you?"

"I've been over in England until last weekend. Haven't talked to him in weeks and he hasn't written. Felt guilty about his progress on the new book, I'll wager. But I gather from the letter he's finished it. Thank God. A posthumous Pendleton should sell like hot cakes."

"You said who is it this time? What do you mean by that?"

Dellevand shrugged. "Arthur got romantic ideas almost every full moon. Generally, they ebbed like the tide."

"Can you name some of the more recent ones?"

Dellevand looked aghast. "Good heavens, man, I'd gotten to where I never paid any attention. And he didn't always tell me their names—he was prone to describe his lady loves in such phrases as the lily maid of Astalot, my lady of the lake. It was the pure ham in him. A writer needs it, too, just as an actor."

And that, with variations, was all we got from them so

64

we sent them off to do their thing with Captain Granger while we got on with the rest of our portion of the three hundred and eight. It got duller and duller as the day wore on, even a second quick chat with Pomfret about his banquet arranging story.

"But they did call me. That's where I was." The golden eyes gleamed with sincerity. "They couldn't find Fenster and he'd forgotten entirely to locate the microphones and the spotlight. The mikes were a fairly simple proposition, I had them spaced along the head table, but the spot was a different matter. It was supposed to pick out people here and there at all the tables, on cue, and it had to be high enough and far enough away . . ."

"Okay, okay," I said wearily. "We'll check with the functions manager."

"That's fine with me," said Pomfret stubbornly, "because that's where I was and the man surely won't lie about it."

After dinner, while Brenda and Antoinette watched television, I sat at the kitchen table and read up on venereal diseases.

According to this Dr. Nicholas J. Fiumara, the origin of syphilis is shrouded in the mists of antiquity, but it appeared in epidemic proportions in western Europe in 1493 and raged furiously for a few decades. It was generally believed that Columbus' crew contracted syphilis from the natives of Hispaniola because, when they returned to Spain from the first voyage, they brought back with them the "Indian measles."

Said the doctor, "Although the 'Columbus theory' of origin has been accepted without question for generations, it is hardly tenable today. There is increasing evidence that syphilis and related treponematoses had been epidemic in Europe, Asia and Africa for centuries and had reached epidemic proportions during the lass movements or armies and populations at the end of the fifteenth and the beginning of the sixteenth centuries."

A history lesson, to boot. He went on, "Gonorrhea is the most prevalent of the five venereal diseases, is worldwide in distribution, and is also the oldest. Description of this disease many be found in the fifteenth chapter of the Book of Leviticus (written about 1500 B.C.). Gonorrhea was known to Hippocrates (400 B.C.) who called it 'strangury,' but it was Galen (A.D. 130), the Greek physician practicing in Rome, who called it gonorrhea. Prevalent in Europe during the fifteenth century, gonorrhea was brought to America by Columbus' crew, who cohabited with the brown maidens and infected them with this disease. In return, the crew were infected with 'Indian measles' caused by a virulent strain of treponema pallidum."

The doctor cited facts and figures: From 1919 through 1939, cases of syphilis and gonorrhea were reported to the Public Health Service each year by at least forty states. By 1939, syphilis was a reportable disease in all of the United States and gonorrhea in all but one. In the United States there was a slow but steady increase in reported cases of gonorrhea and syphilis from 1919 to 1935. Then, in 1936 there was a sharp upward trend in reported syphilis. That was the result, according to Dr. Fiumara, of the establishment of a national venereal disease control program, with a resulting widespread increase in case-finding activities. The peak reached in 1943 represents the result of testing several million men for selective service.

In 1946, the number of cases of gonorrhea exceeded the total number of cases of syphilis for the first time since 1921, and gonorrhea has continued to be reported more frequently than syphilis. In the United States, reported cases of syphilis reached a peak in 1947 and then began a precipitous decline which lasted for almost a decade. The year 1958 saw the first increase in infectious syphilis and each year for the next decade the cases continued to increase. However, fiscal years 1966, 1967 and 1968 witnessed a slight drop each year in reported cases of infectious syphilis. This may mean, Dr. Fiumara reasoned, that the national campaigns against infectious syphilis are bearing fruit and "we can expect a continued reduction in syphilis."

"Knute, Antoinette and I are having some iced coffee. Do you want some, too?" It was Brenda speaking, she'd come into the kitchen while I was reading.

"Huh? Oh, no thanks. You can get me a beer, though."

"What are you reading?"

"Just doing some homework." I grinned to her and went back to my pamphlet. Harking back to a reduction in the disease, the doctor went on, "However, tempering this optimistic interpretation is the realization that more than half a million young men have been taken out of the civilian population and sent to Vietnam. There, some are making their contribution to the military disease statistics. What will happen to reported cases of syphilis when they return to civilian life?" asked Dr. Fiumara.

His next set of statistics stated that since the year 1958 there has been about a 202.9 per cent rise in infectious syphilis in the United States. And, he said, considering that private physicians report only about 11 per cent of their cases of primary and secondary syphilis, "the true incidence of infectious syphilis is seen to be of staggering magnitude. It is estimated by the Public Health Service that the true incidence of infectious syphilis in the United States is about 80,000 cases per year. This is the number of people who can spread the disease in a community. The prevalence of syphilis, that is, the number of new and old syphilis patients who need treatment is about two million persons. During the fiscal year 1968, about 20 per cent of all reported cases were in young people 15 to 19 years of age." He added, however, that syphilis is reported most frequently in the young adult, 20 to 24; then the older young adult, 25 to 29; and then the teen-ager previously mentioned.

He had some grim figures about gonorrhea, too. In 1968, there were 431,380 cases reported in the States. "This represents the largest number of cases ever reported in the history of the United States." Young adults again rank first, the 20- to 24-year-olders; followed by the teen-agers and then the 25 to 29 group.

Now he got down to diagnosis and treatment of syphilis. Syphilis, he said, may be spread in one of five methods: 1. sexual exposure. About 95 per cent of all syphilis is transmitted sexually. 2. Kissing a person who has lesions of primary or secondary syphilis. 3. Prenatally. In 1968, the number of infants infected in the utero was three times as great as in 1960. 4. Transfusion . . . rarely seen today because of the stringent requirement that all blood donors must have a nonreactive blood test. 5. Accidental direct inoculations.

Mein jumped up on the table and sat in the middle of the pamphlet. "Get down, cat," I told him and gave him a push. He wouldn't be moved, hunkered down on the paper and stared at me. "All right," I said, and got up to open a can of food for him.

I sat again and found my place. "Diagnosis presents little difficulty," to quote the doctor. "The drug of choice is penicillin. In our clinics we use an aqueous suspension of procaine penicillin G, giving 600,000 units by intramuscular injection daily or every other day for ten doses."

Then he went into detail of treatment for persons who couldn't come to the clinic every day, for those sensitive to penicillin and post-treatment practices. I gathered that treatment was complicated and of considerable duration. Gonorrhea treatment was just as complicated, maybe more so.

I turned the page, almost knocked over the glass of beer Brenda had left me and, thus reminded, drank from it. Dr. Fiumara took a dim view of VD control until present control methods could be improved. He called for public education "aimed at motivating persons who have exposed themselves to seek early medical care. "Unfortunately," he commented, "with the exception of the military population very little popular education is carried out today, principally because of inadequate budgets and insufficient funds for hiring competent professional educators." I grinned wryly. The same old money problem rears its ugly head.

"Good night, Knute," called Antoinette from the living room.

"Good night," I answered automatically, and turned to the last page. The doctor concluded, rather sadly, I thought, "Syphilis is not only a medical problem; it also has social and moral connotations. Thus, the search for a remedy cannot be confined to clinic and public health medicine but must be shared by other disciplines.

"Today, the fashionable word in public health circles is 'eradication.' It impresses the legislators who hold the

purse strings; it provides the press with intriguing specula-
tion, and it reassures the public who want to hear good
news. Yet the 'good news' complex may be a costly luxury; eradication is the final step of a sequence of in-
creasingly complex actions.

"The first step is control, which reduces the incidence
of a disease to an acceptable level. The second is elimina-
tion, i.e., the causative agent persists but it either does not
cause or very rarely causes human disease. Clinical polio
is a good example; it has not occurred in Massachusetts
for the past four years. The disease, therefore, has been
eliminated from our state, but it has not been eradicated;
the organism still persists.

"The final step is eradication, in which both the causative organism and the disease cease to exist in the geo-
graphic area defined. With the tools clinic and public
health medicine we have at hand today, syphilis can be
controlled, the first step toward eradication."

"Knute, aren't you coming to bed?" Now Brenda
was speaking to me again and I answered, "I'll be right
along." There was one more paragraph.

"Gonorrhea, however, remains the uncontrolled and un-
controllable disease. Our failure to control both gonorrhea
and syphilis prompts questions, which, like spring rain
upon a seeded field, forces the subject to grow. Gonorrhea and syphilis have again caught the attention of clinic
and public health medicine and out of this springs our
hope of eventual control."

I read aloud his final remark, a quotation from Seneca, "A disease is farther on the road to being cured when it breaks forth from concealment," and I thought how much better off Arthur Glenn Pendleton would have been had he gone to a physician who could have told him his fears were groundless. Or even, had they not been, have offered proper cure. What a damnable thing to do to a man—make him believe he had a disease he couldn't bear to tell anyone about. Make him believe it because he'd been primed to buy such a monstrosity. The one guy in a million who wouldn't run to his nearest clinic and check it out—and then sit back and watch him suffer.

And that's what someone had done, I was certain of it. But what I thought didn't matter very much because it was ruled a suicide and Captain Granger let the whole writing barnyard, very strange birds, fly the coop.

I was drinking a cup of very bad coffee at my desk when my phone rang. "Severson," I said into it and grimaced over the coffee's aftertaste.

"Knute? This is Dolph Smith. The damnedest thing, it will be in tomorrow's paper—you know those people Pendleton left his money to? The Clementses of Tarrytown, New York?"

"Yes. What about them?"

"It just came over the AP wire and I swear I don't get it. It seems they didn't know the man. Not at all."

"What? I don't get you."

"The Clementses. They never met him, talked to him, wrote to him, anything. They knew who he was, of course, and that's all. They claim they know of no reason whatsoever that he would leave them a million bucks."

I stared at the mouthpiece. "Well, I'll be damned."

Dolph's voice sharpened. I could almost hear the transition from friend to *Herald Traveler* reporter. "You haven't got any ideas on it, have you? Something the boys in blue are hiding from the public? Like the lady was his mistress—I don't think she could be his illegitimate daughter, she's close to fifty according to the story and Pendleton wasn't that old, he couldn't have had a fifty-year old daughter . . ."

"Dolph, I swear to you, I haven't got a clue."

His breezy manner returned. "Well, if you come across one, remember your pals."

"I will." What the devil, I was thinking, why would a man leave a million dollars to utter strangers?

After Parks and I had breakfast the next morning, I hung around until the paperback bookstore opened. Then I went in and bought copies of all the Arthur Glenn Pendleton books they had on hand.

No better time ever to catch up on my reading. Including the article in the morning *Herald* headlined PENDLETON FORTUNE COMPLETE SURPRISE TO TARRYTOWN COUPLE. The Associated Press writer had asked the question "How did he pick his heirs? At random, from a phone book?"

There was a picture above the caption, an ordinary looking couple, he wearing glasses, she with a posed smile, holding a little child in her lap. A family portrait one might find in a thousand albums. Undistinguished.

I studied the plain middle-aged face of Virginia Clements. What in the name of God could have caused Arthur Glenn Pendleton to leave her a million dollars?

"My goodness," breathed Antoinette, eyes wide. "Isn't that interesting?"

"There was a television show several years ago"— Brenda spoke from the kitchen where she was preparing my lunch—"called 'The Millionaire,' if I remember correctly. He'd give a million dollars to strangers if they'd promise not to tell where it came from. They had to be deserving in some way. And needy."

"That part fits, anyway," Antoinette reported. "They can use the money." She referred to the paper. "It seems they have this little child with a birth defect."

I didn't bother to comment, went out on the balcony with *Backward, Turn Backward* by Arthur Glenn Pendleton, and stretched out on the chaise. Mein appeared and jumped on my stomach, curled up and went to sleep.

The book took place in the Middle West and was about a father and son. Pomfret had said this book was the one that was set in Liberal, Kansas, only it didn't call it that. The name of the town was Clayville and the names of the father and son were Paul Clay and Phillip Clay, Paul being the father.

Paul, the father, was afraid that his son, Phillip, was a sissy. I'd gotten that far when Brenda called me to eat. When I'd finished, I went back to the book and read how his father fixed Phillip up with a prostitute to get him going on certain manly arts when the phone rang and Brenda called, "Knute, it's for you."

I groaned, got up and answered it.

"Detective Severson? Zelinda Pendleton here. I'm coming to see you so don't run off. I'll be there in about fifteen minutes."

"Now, hold it a minute, Mrs. Pendleton. How did you get my address . . . ?"

"From that Smith fellow on the *Herald*. He said to tell you you'd be very interested in what I have to say. And then he said something about not forgetting pals."

"He did, did he?" We'd changed our phone to an unlisted number right after the wedding. Fat lot of good it was going to do if Dolph Smith was passing it around. But, on the other hand, I might be interested in whatever Zelinda Pendleton had to say. "Well, come on then. Do you know how to find the place?"

Of course she did, she said condescendingly, and she did because she arrived on schedule and to my surprise, June Carr was with her.

"Come in," I invited. Zelinda had on blue jeans that fitted over her ample hips and around her sturdy thighs like a second skin. With them she wore a short-sleeved tee shirt with a big peace sign painted on its expansive front and on her feet, thong sandals. She was quite a sight.

June Carr had on a silky pants suit painted all over with pink posies. A study in contrasts in every way.

Brenda greeted them cordially and Antoinette welcomed them like long lost friends. I sat back and waited for Zelinda to launch whatever campaign she had in mind. I didn't have to wait long.

"Junie and I have joined forces," she announced in a voice that could be heard four floors below on the wharf. "We're going to break that ridiculous will wide open."

"I simply cannot understand it. To have committed suicide without changing that will . . . especially when he'd asked me to marry him." Junie blinked her myopic baby-blue eyes. "And if I'd known how badly he treated Zelinda after she gave him ten years of her life . . . He must have been mentally ill. That's clearly the only explanation."

"He was as mad as hell at me after the divorce," Zelinda explained to the world at large. "Held a grudge, Penn was good at that. But I'm no fool, whether I look it or not. We've got ourselves a good lawyer. He says that dollar bit will work to our advantage. Smells of spite, you know. And those nitwits in Tarrytown. Giving that story to the newspapers that they didn't even know him. Evidence, all of it, that his head wasn't right when he made the thing out."

"The funeral was so sad." Junie Carr was perhaps thinking about another crying jag, her wide eyes seemed to blur over. "Hardly anyone at all was there. Not even important newspaper people. Just Zelinda and I and his publisher and Derek Pomfret. You'd think if he were so eager to be buried out there, somebody from the town would have come. It was his home town, and after all, he was famous."

"Brenda," I interjected, "would you please bring the box of Kleenex from the bedroom?" If I knew Junie Carr at all, we were going to have waterworks.

"Why do you think he left his money to those people— what were their names?" Cousin Antoinette asked with interest.

Zelinda laughed, a bark of a laugh. "Oh, I know why all right. He was the father of that kid, you can't fool me. I know Penn too well. Got mixed up with that Clements woman and got her pregnant. Thought he'd make the grand gesture—but not until he'd had the full pleasure of having his money all to himself. Peanuts, that's all I got for alimony. Peanuts. If I hadn't money of my own, I'd have starved to death."

"Oh!" Junie's eyes filled and I passed her the tissue box Brenda had fetched.

"She doesn't like to hear me talk that way about him." Zelinda spoke as though June were deaf and dumb. "But

77

she believes it, too. What other reason could there be? Penn wasn't the type to make a stupid, quixotic play like that."

I picked up the newspaper and looked at the child. I couldn't tell if it was a boy or a girl, it just looked like a baby. "Is it a he? How old is he?"

"It's a boy all right." Zelinda sneered. "A year old. They had the nerve to name him Junior. I'll bet she's got nerves on her nerves, that Clements woman. She's got to have some idiot husband if he doesn't smell a dead rat in the woodpile now."

Antoinette leaned forward, spoke thoughtfully, "But wouldn't that injure your case? I mean, if you prove that the boy is his son?"

Zelinda snorted. "Don't intend to prove it in court. Just plan to spell it out to her. If the boy is his, and I'm damned sure it is, we'll give her enough to take care of the kid. All she has to do is forgo any claims to the estate. We'll take care of the rest and her husband will never know."

"We were going to have a son," June sniffled. "He said that was his sole ambition, to have a son to carry on his name."

"Oh, dear." Antoinette reached over and patted her shoulder. "That is sad."

"Just what do you want with me?" I asked warily.

"I don't care for your Captain Granger nor your Detective Pinkerton. Not an ounce of understanding in either of them. I wanted the name of a policeman I could trust so I went to that Smith fellow, he interviewed me right after Penn's death, did a good job, too. Did you see it in the paper?"

I nodded. Picture and all. One of Dolph's more sensational efforts.

"Well, I asked him and he gave me your name. He said you had a bleeding heart and a bulldog tenacity. That's some combination, if I may say so. Anyway, I want to find out about this Clements child. I called the woman myself and she refused to talk to me. So I suppose it has to be done officially with the power of the fuzz behind it. That's what I want you to do." And she leaned back in the throne-backed wicker chair that had never seemed particularly fragile until she sat in it.

"Why should I do that? I haven't any authority. Not unless it had something to do with his death . . ."

"Maybe it did! She could have been the one who gave him that damnable drug. How do you know she isn't syphilitic?"

"I think social disease is a much nicer phrase," protested Antoinette.

I cut in, "Now hold it." Zelinda Pendleton with the bit between her teeth was capable of moving mountains. "He wasn't infected, you've got to remember that. You can't have both ends against the middle. If he was the father of the little boy, and if she did have VD, it's next to impossible that he wouldn't have contracted it. But he didn't—and he never had been infected, Doc Albert determined that. Not congenitally or any other way."

Zelinda gave me a sudden, shrewd look. "And I suppose you've wondered about June and me? Well, we've got news for you. We've both had blood tests just for the record and the result was negative. Positively negative."

"We'd guessed it would be," I told her coldly. "That's why we didn't push the point."

"You'd guessed? That's the devil of a way to run a police department."

"It seemed obvious, for the same reason I gave you about Mrs. Clements. He'd been married to you, if you'd had VD, he would have caught it. And if he was intimately involved with Miss Carr . . ."

"Oh!" Junie reached for another Kleenex. "He wasn't —he didn't. He treated me like a goddess on a pedestal!"

"All right, all right. Forget that angle," said Zelinda impatiently. "All it will take from you is a phone call— although she might not talk over the phone, a visit would be better. You run over to Tarrytown and dig up the dirt about that Clements boy. And I can guarantee it had something to do with his death. Somehow! I can smell it."

I made my tone as patient as possible. "The Boston police have no authority in New York State. If we wanted the information, we'd have to go through the Tarrytown authorities. If I telephoned Mrs. Clements, she'd have every right in the world to refuse to tell me. And as for going out there, the Boston Police Department does not have funds to send their detectives on wild goose chases."

The green eyes didn't waver. "You get a couple of days off every so often, don't you? Drive out, you'll be there in a few hours. I'll pay your expenses with something to boot."

"Oh, why don't you, Knute?" Antoinette piped up. "I'm so very curious—and because I was sitting right outside when it happened, I feel guilty. I don't think I'll ever really rest until I find out what happened to Arthur Glenn Pendleton."

"I know without asking that Captain Granger would never go for it." I couldn't really blame Antoinette for her interest. My unanswered questions were bugging me, too. But Granger would say it wasn't our problem. I could hear him, "Moses on the mountain, Knute, we've got better things to do right here. The man died accidentally. The why of it isn't any of our business any more."

"On your time off? Unofficially?" Zelinda was pressing.

"Unofficially? But what if Mrs. Clements won't talk to me?"

Zelinda smiled, an unexpected sort of smile with a tinge of the courtesan in it. "A handsome man like you? I'll bet you've managed to come up with a lot of unofficial answers in your time."

"I'll think about it." I had Thursday and Friday coming

81

to me and Antoinette was leaving Friday. She'd be out of the house when I got back, a comforting thought. And I might come up with something—just might. "Would you object?" I asked Brenda.

She shook her head. She was good at reading my mind, I knew. I wasn't so apt at reading hers. Was she just being polite or did she really want me to go? I asked her in bed that next morning, whispered so Antoinette wouldn't hear.

"I don't care about helping those women," was Brenda's answer. "They're both rather awful in their way. Anxious for the money, although I suppose that's natural when there's so much of it. But I am curious, just as you are. It seems such a fantastic affair—and a shame somehow. He was a talented writer. Even though he might not have been such a nice man."

"It's a funny thing . . ." I spoke slowly, I'd forgotten about Antoinette and if I woke her up, the hell with it. "I never even saw him, you know, hadn't read any of his books, he was just a name. But I've got this strange reaction coming on . . . I'm beginning to crawl into his skin. No, that's not what I mean. Not exactly. It's as though it was a murder, a true murder, the killing of a man through his manhood. Am I making any sense at all? There's something about the whole business that makes my flesh crawl. I almost feel as though by doing this thing to Pendleton, it was done to me." I stopped talking, I wasn't putting it well. Pendleton would have said it much better.

Brenda raised up on her elbows, smiled at me as a mother might at a child.

"All right," I said crossly, "I know all men are little boys at heart and I'm worse than most. But what makes a man a man is important."

"Of course it is," she agreed sweetly.

"Well, then, don't sound so damned patronizing!" And I lay back and closed my eyes, listened to her get up and get dressed and after a while I went back to sleep.

I reached Tarrytown shortly after 4 P.M. The weather was humid and maybe ten degrees warmer these two hundred miles southwest. The Hudson looked cool, sparkled in the afternoon sun. People said it was badly polluted, but it looked inviting.

I stopped and asked directions from a traffic patrolman who told me how to find the street the Clements lived on. It was around four-thirty when I pulled up in front of a neat little brick house set among a group of similar small houses on a quiet street. Middle-class, well-kept neighborhood, I tabbed it. I got out, walked up a cement walk, climbed four brick steps and rang the doorbell. I heard it sound, bong-bong, inside.

From somewhere deep in the house came the thin wail of an infant and then, approaching footsteps. The door opened and a woman looked out at me. I recognized her from her picture. I said, "Mrs. Clements? My name is Severson. I'm from Boston."

Her light brown hair looked newly washed, was tied back with a length of red ribbon. She was not so plain in person, not as old looking as I'd thought, her skin was nice, slightly tanned, and her dark blue eyes were alive, expressive. Looking at me now they expressed polite curiosity edged with concern.

"From Boston? But . . ."

I showed my identification. "I'm not here officially, I'm off duty. But if you could spare me a few moments of your time . . . ?"

The baby cried again, louder this time. It seemed to fluster her. "Come in, I suppose. Would you please excuse me a moment. The baby . . ." and she let me in, left me in the cool shadows of the hall while she hurried to the back of the house.

I took a few steps forward, to the living room, looked around. Furnished pleasantly enough, the predominate color was beige. Nothing outstanding, ordinary furniture set around in an orderly fashion. Clean. Restrained. Unimaginative.

"I'm sorry," Virginia Clements spoke from the hall. She held an infant over her shoulder, supported his back with one hand, held a baby bottle in the other. "Please sit down. It's his feeding time."

"I'm sorry if I chose an inconvenient moment."

"I'll just feed him while we talk if you don't mind."

"Not at all."

"Sit down, then." She sat herself on the tan-colored sofa, shifted the baby so that she could put the bottle in his mouth. His eyes closed as his mouth closed over the nipple and he began to suck. He looked smaller than I had expected, but then I didn't know much about babies. Parks had a new one, I hadn't even seen it.

"What is it that you wanted, Mr. Severson?" Motherly . . . no, serene was the word for her, I decided. She tended the baby as though she'd been born to the job.

"It's about the Pendleton will."

"I was afraid it was." Her eyes were really quite beautiful, shone with some unusual sort of light. There was something about her . . . perhaps Zelinda had been right. She might have appealed to Pendleton, at that.

"As you no doubt know, Arthur Pendleton died in a hotel in Boston quite suddenly." I seated myself carefully on a rather fragile-looking ladder-back chair. "The circumstances were unusual so his death underwent routine investigation. We know how he died, but we're not sure why."

The baby lost his nipple and fussed. She put the bottle aside, held him against her shoulder and patted his back. He belched loudly. She smiled, put him down again, gave back the bottle. "And you want to know why he left his money to us—well, Mr. Severson, so do we." She looked at me with guileless eyes.

"The papers said—you really have no idea?"

Some emotion, I couldn't identify it, it came and went so quickly, caused her eyes to change color. "None whatsoever," she said levelly. "My husband and I have explored every possibility in our own minds. We simply don't know." She looked down at her baby.

"But it doesn't make sense . . ."

Still watching the baby, "No sense at all."

I aimed for a nerve. "Doesn't that make you reluctant to accept the bequest?"

She looked up, eyes shining. "Oh, no. We consider it a gift from the stars."

"Even though there might be—somehow—a gross error? Some other family named Clements . . . ?"

"Some other family named Franklin Edward Clements and Virginia Hanks Clements?" Her look was almost merry.

"I'll grant you, it seems most unlikely, but then it's no more fantastic than an utter stranger leaving you a million dollars."

She didn't answer. The baby had stopped pulling at the bottle. His eyes were closed, he looked to be asleep. Mrs. Clements put the bottle aside, hauled him up and burped him once more. He cried once, went back to sleep. She went through this process with complete concentration and I watched in bemused fascination.

"Franklin Edward, Jr., is a Leo, you know." Her hands smoothed his blanket as she returned her attention to me. "Franklin, Sr., is an Aries and I am a Gemini. Well-matched, all of us, according to the stars. That's why I said a gift from the stars. Our stars are smiling upon us. They knew Franklin, Junior, needed help and so they swung in their orbits, influenced Mr. Pendleton. I wonder what his Zodiac sign was? I must find out."

"The baby needs help? In what way?" I remembered Zelinda had said something about a birth defect, but so far as I could see he seemed okay.

"Our little boy wasn't born perfect, but with Mr. Pendleton's largess we shall be able to make him that way. Would you like to see?"

I wasn't sure whether I wanted to see or not, but she didn't wait for my answer. She removed the light blanket from the small body and unfastened his rubber pants, unpinned his diaper. Some sort of strange, furious red mass marred the little white stomach. Uncooked meat —I didn't know what. Mrs. Clements solved the mystery in a tone that verged on the proud. "Our little boy was born with his bladder outside his body. The doctors say he will require several operations over the years to correct it. Now we can afford them." She wore a beatific expression. I got the feeling she was in some other world, she and the child.

I stood up. "What business is Mr. Clements in?"

She began to refasten the baby's clothing. "He's a real estate broker."

"What's the name of his company?"

87

She stared at me. "I don't believe I shall tell you. He would only tell you the same as I and he's too busy to be bothered." She picked the baby up and looked at me over his head. "Besides, you really don't have any right to be pestering us, do you? We don't have to answer your questions if we don't want to?"

"No," I told her, "you don't." I left her there, holding the child close, sort of rocking back and forth and crooning a little tune. The Yellow Pages would have the names of Tarrytown realtors. All I needed to do was find a phone booth and start on the Yellow Pages with a bunch of dimes. Which I did, and, as things always seem to go, Clements was employed at the last real estate office I called.

But I was lucky in one respect. He was in.

I cheated. I didn't tell him exactly who I was when I made an appointment to come right over. I had no idea what his attitude would be. At least if I could see him face to face, I could read his expression.

He was the man in the newspaper photograph to a T. Slender, bespectacled, mild-looking. Nobody would glance at him twice.

He studied my identification, then my face. "I suppose it's about the Pendleton business?" His tone was resigned.

"Yes. But unofficially. You're not required to answer my questions."

He handed back my ID, sighed. He had a little cubicle

of an office, so at least we had some privacy. "There's no point in refusing to answer," he said. "For one thing, I have nothing to hide, and for another, I guess it's just part of the price we have to pay."

"Your wife doesn't exactly share your sentiments."

"You've talked to Virginia?"

"I've just come from there."

He looked thoughtful. "She's concerned about the baby. Last night she asked me if all this publicity mightn't be dangerous. Get him kidnapped—something like that."

"Why did you talk to the newspapers in the first place?" They'd been the ones to open the can of worms when they'd said Pendleton was a complete stranger.

"They called and asked me how I felt about the money. I'd never been interviewed before, never did anything to warrant it. I just told them the truth." He put on a slightly surprised expression as though to say, what else would one do?

I did a quick mental rundown on ways to ask the million-dollar question. I came up with "Mr. Clements, in line with our investigation of Pendleton's death, there's one question I have to ask." I paused. I kind of liked the guy. "Is there any question at all in your mind as to whether you're the father of this baby?"

He opened his mouth slightly. I could see his teeth, they were on edge. "None whatever," he told me evenly.

"None whatever?" I stressed the final word.

"None. I know I'm not the child's blood father. But

then neither is Virginia his natural mother. Franklin, Junior, is adopted, you see."

I stared at him. "Adopted? But Mrs. Clements never said . . . she didn't indicate in any way . . ."

"She wouldn't. She'd wanted a child for so long, for years we'd tried to have our own. To tell you the truth, I didn't go for adoption. I thought somehow we could . . . anyway, by the time she'd talked me into it, we had reached the age where they don't like to give you a child. We tried several agencies, all we were getting was a run-around. It was beginning to get Virginia down, I got really worried. So I heard about this place in New York called the Crib and I took a day off and went in . . . well, after interviews with both of us and a lot of rig-marole they said, even though we were over the age limit, they had a little boy just a few days old and we almost went through the roof, we were so happy. Then they told us the catch, he had a birth defect, would we take him with that and I looked at Virginia, her eyes were shining, I've never seen her look so happy, not in years, and I said yes and she said, oh, yes, and that's how we got Franklin Edward, Jr." He grinned shyly. "That's maybe a longer story than you wanted to hear."

"Where did the baby come from? Who were his natural parents?"

"We don't know that. All they told us was the nationality, English and Scotch, similar to ours. The parents were unmarried, they said, but apparently came from decent backgrounds. They never give the names to the adoptive parents nor do they tell the natural parents where the child has gone. That's to keep people from changing their minds. You see how it could be."

The Crib. In New York City, some twenty-five miles away. Maybe they wouldn't tell the adoptive parents but they just might tell me. It was worth trying anyway.

I drove into the city and got a room at the Summit Hotel and called Brenda. Antoinette answered.

"Oh, Knute," she trilled. "Where are you? What did you find out?"

I didn't intend to spell it all out to her. "Nothing much, yet. Is Brenda there?"

"No, she's gone out. Shopping, I think. I expect her back soon. Do you want her to call you?"

Damn! "No, just tell her I'm at the Summit in New York if she needs me. And I should be home tomorrow by late afternoon. What time are you leaving?"

"Harley says he wants to get an early start for the weekend. He'll be by about three."

I made a mental note to time my arrival accordingly. "Have a good trip," I told her.

"Thank you. And thank you again, Knute, for all your kindnesses and hospitality. I've enjoyed myself thoroughly."

"Any time," I said heartily. "Come back and see us any time."

She laughed. "You're really very sweet, but don't worry. I'll be staying put now that I've had my fling. I've got a lot of work to do and there's no place like home to do it in."

What could I say? I said, "Take care of yourself, Antoinette," and she said she would and we made our good-bys. Then I went out and had a good steak dinner and saw a movie. When I got back to the hotel, I read a couple more chapters of *Backward, Turn Backward*. It seemed that the father in the book had some sort of mysterious ailment that he was trying to hide from his son, but his son suspected something was wrong.

I slept pretty soundly considering that I was alone in a strange bed.

The Crib was located in a dressed-up, old-fashioned brownstone on the East Side. It had been someone's home once, I figured. In what had been the formal entrance hall stood a real crib with baby toys in it and with a bird mobile hanging over the top of it. An empty crib, no baby in it. Symbolic, I supposed, of the people who came there with empty cribs.

I told the receptionist who I was. "I'd like to speak to the director, if I may."

She was a motherly-looking type, quite appropriate, with a matronly figure and eyes that squinted a little, eyes that squinted even more at the word detective. "Miss

Cragmore has someone in with her now. If you don't mind waiting . . ."

I said I didn't and took a chair next to a magazine table containing copies of *Parents' Magazine,* the *Reader's Digest* and the like.

I was scanning an article called "Was Dr. Spock Wrong?" when a door down the corridor opened and a couple emerged. They were attractive people, nicely dressed, but they looked uptight. Someone inside the door was saying, "We'll call you, Mrs. Winters, when we have any news."

"Thank you," said the man, presumably Mr. Winters. The door closed and the Winterses came forward, nodded to the receptionist and went out. As they passed the crib, the man poked at one of the mobile birds and the woman said in a choked voice, "Oh, Stan . . ." The outer door closed on them.

The motherly lady picked up a phone and spoke softly into it, listened, spoke some more. When she hung up, she said, "Miss Cragmore will give you a few minutes now."

Miss Cragmore had professional written all over her. Her dark hair was pulled back into a bun arrangement, her clothes were tailored, her skirt length a compromise between knee and thigh. She was thoroughly businesslike in her approach, too. She had an appointment at ten-thirty so she couldn't give me much time. What was it I wanted?

I told her. "I realize that you do not reveal the names of the parents of your charges indiscriminately, but under the circumstances I thought you might be willing to aid this investigation." I hoped I was as businesslike as she.

She sat straighter and placed her efficient-looking hands flat on the desk top. "I'm afraid I can't. The Clements adoption is not yet final. I don't mean to offend your profession, but a leakage of information could be utterly detrimental. . . ."

I bit my lip. If this was Boston and I was on surer ground . . . but I knew damn well I couldn't get a court order. "Naturally, I can't force you." I spoke in what I hoped was a friendly persuading manner. "But perhaps you could tell me just one thing. Perhaps you could tell me if I'm wrong or right when I say that Arthur Pendleton was the father of the Clements baby. You don't have to say anything, just nod yes or no." Even as I spoke, I knew it wouldn't work. I guess if I was in her place, I wouldn't do it either.

"To begin with, Mr. Severson, I don't know offhand who the father was. I would have to go into the files, we serve a great many families and I don't have that information at my finger tips. Secondly, I believe you told me the man died accidentally. I can't see why the paternity of a child has any bearing on his death. Had it been a case of death by violence, if this highly confidential information would have helped bring someone to justice, I might feel differently. But it seems to me that you ask these questions purely to solve your own curiosity. It's far too important to the child to bandy names about. That's who we think of first here at the Crib, the child. First, last and always." She glanced down at her wristwatch. "And now, if you'll excuse me, I believe my next visitors are due."

I got up to go, defeated, but I had another thought and I stopped for a final try. "Who does know the names of the parents of the children here? Other than yourself? Somebody must, it must be a matter of record somewhere and someone must prepare these records."

"The original birth certificates are impounded and new corrected ones are written." She walked around her desk, opened her door for me. Down by the receptionist's desk, I saw another couple waiting. They were holding hands.

"But you haven't answered my question," I argued. "I'm trying to determine if anyone else could have found out. The natural father, for instance. Could he have found out who adopted his child?"

"Impossible," said Miss Cragmore firmly, positively. She gestured toward the couple down the hall. "Won't you come in, please, Mr. and Mrs. Blake?"

Mr. and Mrs. Blake passed me as I walked slowly and thoughtfully away. I had learned to doubt people who made firm and positive statements.

I paused at the receptionist's desk and asked, "How many people are employed here?"

She glanced toward Miss Cragmore's closed door as though she expected that lady to come out and tell her what to answer. "You mean—clerical and social workers?" she asked me back.

I nodded. She squinted and wet her lips nervously. "I guess—maybe ten. Not counting the janitorial help."

"And how many of these are social workers?" There was the key. The social worker, the go-between.

"We did have six—but now we have five. We have five social workers."

I raised my eyebrows, purely for effect. I was fishing, I didn't know for what. "What happened to the sixth?"

"I believe he resigned. A better job, I think. Or maybe the Peace Corps. I'm not really sure." She set her kindly mouth into uncharitable lines to show me she'd gone as far as she could go.

"When? When did he resign?"

"Months ago. I don't remember."

"And his name?"

She squinted until her eyes were nearly closed, then, in an act of defiance, reached for her phone. "Miss Cragmore," she said into it, "I'm sorry to interrupt but this detective is asking me questions . . ."

She listened, nodded, put the phone back in its cradle. "Miss Cragmore says I don't have to talk to you at all."

And so I left the Crib. I'd been fishing in murky waters and came up with an empty line. But there was more than one way to bait a hook. . . .

Hook. Hooked. I was the one who was hooked. For personal reasons I had to find out what had happened to Arthur Glenn Pendleton and it wasn't clear even to me what those personal reasons were.

By the time September rolled around, when the leaves began to turn, I'd investigated three homicides, six robberies, seventeen breaking-and-enterings plus a handful of unclassifiable oddities in the space of a couple of months.

I was tired. And inclined to be irritable. And still bugged by the shade of Arthur Glenn Pendleton.

I'd managed to read his books in my off hours. If there was any of the man in those books, and I guessed there had to be, I'd learned that that man had adored his father, had a love-hate relationship with the women in his life, was an avid sportsman—hunting, fishing, mountain climbing, skiing, sailing, you name it, Pendleton had done it.

The book I liked best was the first one *Backward,* etc. The father in that book, Paul Clay, the one with the mysterious ailment killed himself in the end. The book never did explain what unspeakable disease caused him to take his own life. . . .

He hadn't been able to put it down on paper, to spell it out. I could guess at how the young boy had felt—how I would feel. My father, my own father. The

stigma of it. Pendleton had been able to admit the suicide
. . . if that's what it had been, it seemed to me from his
letter to Dellevand that his father's death could have
been accidental, perhaps that was where the whole ugly
mess had started, that assumption of suicide . . . but not
the cause.

I spent a great deal of time thinking about this paradox.
On every page of the book was this obsession with manly
acts. His father had preached the sermon and Pendleton
had absorbed it like a sponge. Was suicide, therefore, an
act of great courage in his eyes? In some crazy way,
did he believe that VD was an act of manhood?

I thought of my own father. A man. A man to respect,
but a man who was inherently gentle, perhaps even
womanly by Pendleton's standards. His pleasure from
his fussy lodge doings, the little boy joy from dressing
up in a feathered hat.

I guessed there was something wrong about Pendleton's
attitude toward the sexes. Growing up without a mother,
that might do it. But I'd known guys who'd lost their
mothers at an early age—Mert Jacques, for instance. My
one-time and late lamented partner. Mert had learned
housekeeping chores as a boy, many's the time I'd seen
him in an apron, drying dishes for his wife . . . why
did this bother me so? Was I still trying to find out my
personal role? Would I dry dishes for Brenda if she
asked me to? And if not, why not?

Zelinda Pendleton and June Carr had instituted their

suit, even though I came back from Tarrytown next to empty-handed. It hadn't come to court yet but at the time it was filed there was a flurry in the newspapers about it and Virginia Clements was quoted as saying, "Let them sue us. We have faith in the stars."

I'd come to a real dead end in the paternity of the baby business. I'd gone so far as to pay a visit to Phoebe Scott, an old acquaintance in the State Division of Child Guardianship in the vain hope that she might be able to come up with some new avenues to explore. But no soap. Which was as it should be, I guess. Phoebe and I hadn't exactly hit it off the first time we met, which was a few years back when we were dealing with a case in which a foster child was shut in an old refrigerator.

And so, I'd begun to play pen and pencil games with myself on fall evenings. Brenda would be reading or watching the TV with Mein for company and I'd sit at the kitchen table making lists:

Known facts—suspicions—possibilities—impossibilities.

Under known facts about all I could write was that Arthur G. Pendleton died following an injection of arsphenamine. Died alone, locked in his hotel room with Antoinette Evers sitting outside. Supposedly by his own hand. Supposedly in his right mind.

Under faint possibilities I asked, could Antoinette have gotten into and out of the room leaving the doors locked?

This was a possibility that had occurred to me at the

time of his death, but it was no go because Pinkerton had carefully noted that the connecting bathroom door's lock was snapped on the inside and Pomfret definitely had the only available key to the door that opened onto the sitting room, had produced it upon his return after the discovery of the body. So no matter how I reasoned it might have gone—i.e., Pomfret didn't leave the door locked (either by accident or design) thus permitting Antoinette to enter the bedroom . . . only how could she relock the door without a key? It required a key to lock it.

And ditto for the door being locked as advertised, neither Antoinette nor Pendleton himself could have unlocked it—not without that key.

So that left the snap lock on the connecting door and the only possibility that was even remote was that Pendleton had let Antoinette—or someone else—in that way, let them out again and relocked that door. But why?

On the subject of "or someone," if there was a someone, then Antoinette had to be lying in her teeth when she said no one entered the suite, no one at all. Pinkerton's notes and my personal observation bore out the fact that this had been truly a suite, both bedrooms opened onto the sitting room and not on a hall. You'd have to come through that sitting room. Have to. It was so high up, the windows were an impossibility.

But someone had brought him the arsphenamine. He'd said they would in his letter—Pomfret had sworn Pendleton hadn't brought it with him.

June Carr? I couldn't believe it. Besides, according to witnesses, she'd been elsewhere, hadn't seen him, gone near the twenty-sixth floor.

Zelinda? Came in from Plymouth? Physically possible —except that Pomfret and Antoinette bore witness to the fact that he hadn't seen her—hadn't seen anyone.

Damn it!

Did Pendleton know who had adopted his son? Someone from the Crib would have had to tell him. Damn Miss Cragmore! I'd even written her a letter spelling this out and she'd written back one paragraph. "The implication is an insult to our dedicated staff. Because we are human, I presume we are all capable of sins of omission and commission. But in this, the first and most vital of our commandments, I say to you, sir, impossible." Signed, (Miss) Pamela Cragmore.

And I'd crumpled it in anger and thrown the letter into the wastebasket, barely missing the perambulating cat as I did so. Impossible? My foot!

If the Clements baby was Pendleton's son—who was the mother? I had a Xerox of the list of more than three hundred persons at the Creative Writing shindig. I'd studied their statements, the ones Parks and I took and all the others as well. I couldn't point a finger at any of the women and even say maybe. Especially not June Carr. I said a definite no to that for many reasons, not the least of which was the M.D.'s report she and Zelinda had arbitrarily given to Captain Granger. June Carr, according to medical evidence, had never given birth. Neither had Zelinda Pendleton. The latter was already through the menopause and the former had a tipped uterus which made pregnancy, in the words of the doctor, "extremely unlikely without corrective surgery."

Suddenly irritated, I slammed the papers together and stood up. Stalking into the living room I said to Brenda, "What are you watching?"

Brenda glanced up, answered, "Marcus Welby," and Mein yawned. "Are you through with your homework?" Brenda asked.

"It wasn't homework. Just some foolishness." I plunked myself into a chair, tried to concentrate on the TV.

"We got some mail today. A letter from your mother and father. I'll get it for you."

That irritated me, too. "Why didn't you tell me?"

"I'm sorry. I forgot." She handed me an envelope, one of two.

"Who's the other from?"

"Antoinette."

"Oh?" I reached up. "Aren't you going to let me read it?"

"I didn't think you'd be especially interested."

"Well, I am."

She turned quickly away and I felt ashamed of myself. "Brenda—I'm sorry. I've been a bastard lately, haven't I?" I reached out and caught her hand.

"Somewhat." She smiled, a small smile. I pulled her close, down onto my lap.

"Forgive me." I kissed her.

"I forgive you," she whispered, and we kissed again. Then I gave her a playful push. "Up. I want to read."

"You can't do that!" shouted Marcus Welby from the TV screen.

"I'll turn the television off," Brenda offered.

"No, I'll go into the kitchen." And I did.

Mom and Dad were fine. Dad was growing tomatoes and oranges on their Florida property. Mom had discovered the joys of a ladies' shuffleboard club. Shud-up, the dog, liked to run the beach. Everything was going well. Thank God.

I opened Antoinette's letter. It was written in a spidery sort of hand that somehow surprised me. Despite her age, there was something so childlike about Antoinette in person, but her handwriting looked old. I had trouble making it out.

She was responding, apparently, to a letter from Brenda. She said yes, she was feeling fine and working hard at her writing. She'd had a couple of poems accepted by a Canadian newspaper. "They don't pay, of course, but it's good exposure."

"You asked me about Doreen," the letter continued on a new subject. "She is literally blooming. Truly, Brenda, there has never been a lovelier child. All the boys for miles around come courting and she is kind to all, but most particular. I tell her that her young Lochinvar will come out of the West if she is patient. She makes me feel nineteen again, just to look at her. She reminds me of my first love—oh, that was so long ago! And how we planned to marry and live in a Spanish castle. Of course it never came true for me, but the dream was worth the dreaming. I would be a very happy old woman if my Doreen could take my place in that dream."

I called to Brenda, "Who is Doreen?"

"Uncle Forrest's daughter. Antoinette's niece. She's the apple of her eye," came the reply from the living room.

I finished the letter. Antoinette thanked us again for our hospitality and said some nice things about me and urged Brenda to write soon. I put the sheets back in their envelope and yawned involuntarily. I was tired, could be that accounted for my lousy disposition. I had a couple of days coming to me the end of the week. Maybe Brenda and I could go off someplace, the Cape? Mrs. Baldau downstairs would look after the cat. I stretched, got up and turned out the light.

I walked into the living room, held out my arms. "Come to bed," I said, "and I'll tell you how much I love you."

On Thursday, I asked Brenda, "How far is it to that town where Antoinette lives?"

She looked surprised. "Vale, Vermont? A six- or seven-hour drive, I should think. Why?"

"How would you like to drive up and visit her tomorrow? We could stay overnight at a motel, have a change of scene. I've never been up that way before."

Brenda studied me for a moment, lowered her lashes. "I suppose we could. It should be lovely and cool up there. But I'd better call and tell her we're coming . . ."

"Better yet, let's surprise her," I said gently, but firmly. "Antoinette impresses me as the type who loves surprises."

Brenda glanced up, looked down again just as quickly. I added hurriedly, "And as long as we won't be putting her out by needing bed or board. . . ."

"No, we wouldn't be putting her out . . ." she murmured, seemed about to say something else but didn't, which was just as well. I had a hunch she'd been about to ask a question and even I wasn't too sure why I wanted to drive up to Vale. I only knew I did.

Brenda was right, it was cooler, maybe ten degrees or more in the north country. The scenery was nice, too, grass, trees and lots of cows. Not too much traffic after we got away from the metropolitan areas. The sun shone through tree-lined roadways, the air was fresh. I found myself humming under my breath. A good, golden day was worth humming about.

"Knute . . ." Brenda leaned back against the seat, eyes hidden behind sunglasses.

"Huhm? Hey, look at that bird! Bright blue. An indigo bunting, I'll bet. I've never seen one before except in a bird book."

"Where? Oh, he's lovely." She was silent for a moment, then, "Knute, you're still thinking about Arthur Glenn Pendleton, aren't you?"

"What brought that up?"

"You tucked one of his books in the overnight bag."

"He's an interesting writer. Had a lot of interests. Hunting. Fishing. Skiing. Mountain climbing, canoeing, went all over pursuing his hobbies. Very masculine stuff."

Her head was down. I thought she was studying her fingers. The half-carat diamond I'd been able to afford glittered in the sun. "Does this trip have anything to do with Pendleton?"

I considered before I answered. My impulse was to say no, but I wasn't sure. Dangerous ground. Brenda's relative. I decided my instincts were right. "Not a thing," I said cheerily. "Just striking out in a different direction—and glad I did. Look at that view!"

She looked. "Yes. It is gorgeous, isn't it?"

Vale appropriately enough lay in a valley. We looked down on it from the roadway, saw the pristine spire of a church and, on the road below us, what appeared to be a covered bridge. "A mighty pretty town," I thought aloud.

"Yes." Brenda smiled. "I'd forgotten. I haven't been here since I was a girl."

"You're still a girl," I told her and we headed down,

across the covered bridge. Somehow, I felt as though we were moving back in time. It wasn't a bad feeling.

The Vale Inn stood between the Episcopalian church and the Town Hall. The inn was a white-shingled and rambling building, its small-paned windows held leaded glass.

Our room was a corner one shaded by a tall elm and a stately oak. The furnishings looked to me to be real antiques, but Brenda said they were reproductions, good reproductions. The bed had a red calico canopy to match its ruffled spread and the curtains at the windows were of the same material. A little fussy, maybe, but a charming place just the same. I sighed and sat in the easy chair, looking out the window. Brenda, hanging up things from the overnight bag asked if I wanted to lie down for a while. "You must be tired. It was a long drive."

"Nope." The post office was across the street and next to that was a drugstore with red and green bottles in the windows. "We don't have time."

She paused in the act of putting something in a bureau drawer. "Don't have time?"

I grinned at her. "We've only got a night and part of tomorrow. How am I going to see everything in Vale, Vermont, if I spend it in bed? A big place like this?"

She laughed. "All right, city boy. But small towns have their advantages. In Boston or New York, you could break your leg in the bathtub and starve to death before anybody knew you were missing."

I gave her a mock scowl. "And in places like Vale, Vermont, everybody knows your business."

She closed the bureau drawer, put the suitcase in the closet. "I may have been exaggerating about Boston, but you're telling the truth about small towns. Everybody's had a look at the skeletons in the closets."

A man and woman came out of the post office and went into the drugstore. A group of teen-agers came down the street. No hippie types in Vale. The boys had short hair and the girls wore pastel dresses.

"I'll wash my face and hands," said Brenda, "and then I'll be ready. Where do you want to go first?"

"Hummm? Oh, to Antoinette's, I guess. Unless it's too close to dinnertime. Should we eat first?"

From the bathroom, she answered in muffled tones, "Isn't it early for dinner? It's only five-thirty."

"I guess you're right." The post office was closing, someone was locking the door. A woman by the shape of her. Probably Antoinette's nosy postmistress. "I could use a drink to unwind. Do you suppose they have any bars in this place?"

"I don't know, I suppose so. I was underage my last visit, but, yes, I'm sure they do. I thought I saw a cocktail lounge downstairs on the way in."

I pushed myself up out of my chair. A Volkswagen van came down the street, pulled up in front of the store beyond the drugstore, a market, according to the sign outside. Bertrand's Market. A man and two little girls got out

of the van and went into the market. The next door beyond that was being locked by a man in a light-colored
suit. Closing up time in Vale, I gathered. Three cars
passed going west, two others went east. A nice quiet
little town.

"Are you ready?" asked Brenda at the door.

"Yep. Got the key?"

"Here." She handed it to me and we went out into the
hall, walked along an oriental runner to the staircase that
led down to the lobby and the desk. The desk clerk, a very
neat middle-aged type with a small moustache and a carna-
tion in his lapel was reading a newspaper. He looked up
as we approached, asked affably, "Room all right?"

"Fine, thank you," Brenda told him.

"Is the cocktail lounge open?" I inquired.

"Yes, indeed. It opens at four." He turned the page
of his newspaper with an efficient snap. "Gives Clifford
time to polish up the glasses. Most customers don't come
in till about six. Quitting time, you know."

"In that case, we'll drop in and keep Clifford company."
I aimed Brenda in the right direction, to the left where an
old English sign spelled out the letters Pub Room. The
desk clerk rattled his paper behind us, but I got the idea
he was watching us. I turned to see, but all I got was a
local headline: MILDRED ABBOTT WINS 4-H
AWARD.

The Pub Room was dark paneled, naturally, and cozy.
Clifford, I presumed it was he, stood polishing glasses

behind a shiny bar. Crisp red curtains framed the dia-mond-pane windows and damned if the place didn't have two Tiffany lamp shades in stained glass colors.

We picked out a table and sat down. Clifford stopped polishing and ambled over. He was youngish, heavy set with sandy hair and thick eyebrows.

"Afternoon," said Clifford. "What can I do for you folks?"

I looked at Brenda, she nodded and I ordered two gim-lets. Clifford nodded cheerfully and made his way back to the bar. "You folks want some music?" he asked. "Or do you want to watch the television? Nothing much on at this time, except the news. In my opinion, that's always so depressing, I don't bother to turn the button."

"Music will do just fine," I told him. He nodded, even more cheerfully, and turned a switch on the wall. Soft strains from hidden loud speakers played something I couldn't identify, but it was pleasant. "This is a nice place you've got here," I told Clifford.

"First class," he responded, nodding his head know-ingly. "They built a motel out the other side of town couple of years ago, but folks tell me it doesn't hold a candle to the old inn." He completed his mixology chore, came around the bar with two glasses on a tray. "You folks new around here, aren't you?"

I took one of the gimlets and tasted it. It was excellent. "Just visiting," I told him. "A relative of my wife's. Maybe you know her. Antoinette Evers?"

"Miss Evers? Sure, I know her. Everybody knows Miss Evers. Mighty fine lady. Comes from a real old Vale family, guess maybe her family was one of the first in the valley." He held out his hand. "My name's Clifford Allison. Pleased to meet some relatives of Miss Evers."

"Severson," I said, shaking his hand. "My wife, Brenda." Brenda smiled. "Miss Evers is her cousin."

"Severson." He repeated the name, pumped my hand again. "Welcome to Vale in the valley of Eden." He grinned sheepishly. "That's what they call it in the weekly newspaper. Chamber of Commerce stuff. But it is mighty nice."

"Mighty nice," I echoed. He nodded again and went back to his bar. The music changed to, of all things, "Stardust."

"What's the best place to eat around here, Clifford?" I asked after a few minutes.

"Why, right here at the inn. Real good fare. Only, Miss Evers, won't she be cross as two sticks if you eat dinner out? She's great on hospitality is Miss Evers."

Brenda gave me a look. I said, "Well, you see, we've come from Boston to surprise her and we didn't want to surprise her that much."

Clifford, who had resumed his polishing, paused with glass and towel in hand. "From Boston?" He knotted his brow in concentration. "If I recall, she has got some folks in Boston, spent some time with them awhile back." His frown went away and he began polishing once more.

"You must be the policeman, then. Miss Evers said her niece was married to some big Boston policeman. Niece? Or was it her cousin?"

"Cousin. Yes, I would be the policeman." In an aside to Brenda, I added, "News does get around in a small town."

"It was in the Vale *Sentinel*." Clifford started on a new glass. "An interview with Miss Evers. All about that writer fellow dying and all."

"Oh, I see." I'd finished my drink but when I looked over, Brenda had hardly touched hers. "How about a re-fill, Clifford? Just for me."

"Sure thing."

"What did Antoinette say about Pendleton's death?" I asked conversationally.

"Oh, what a great writer he was and what a shame that he had to die so young. How he got hold of some old medicine, a tragic accident, that's what she called it." He poured the gimlet into a fresh glass, came toward me with it. "Course, he may have seemed young to her, but I didn't think of him as being all that young. His hair was kinda gray and all. Died in his prime, the paper said. Betty Pine, she's the society editor and she wrote the story, she gets pretty fancy with words every so often."

"Did you know Pendleton?" I asked carefully.

"Why, sure I did. He spent more'n a month up here a couple of years ago. Fishing. You may not know it but we got some of the finest trout streams in the country. Landlocked salmon, too, out in Vale Lake. You just drop in a line and—whoosh! You got yourself maybe a twelve-inch brookie. Pendleton was a fishing fiend. Couple of times he brought in enough to feed the whole inn."

I didn't dare look at Brenda. "Guess I'll have to try that myself one day."

"If you need a guide, you get ahold of Henry Oliphant. What he don't know about fishing just ain't worth knowing. You know, like if it's not the season, private spots and the like." He winked at me knowingly.

"And where would I find Henry Oliphant?"

"He's the evening man down at Kingman's gas station, right down at the end of Main Street. Works there at night, fishes days. Tell him Clifford sent you. He'll be glad to show you around, specially since you're related to Miss Evers." The doors from the lobby opened and two men came through them. "Evening, Herbie, Jim. How's it going?"

Herbie—or Jim—told him things were okay, or would be as soon as they had the usual. Brenda, in a low voice, said, "Knute I know what you're thinking . . ."

I looked back at her. Her dark eyes were shadowed and she would only return my glance for a moment. "It means something, you know that," I said quietly. "The fact that he was here. Antoinette didn't mention it, not to me. If I remember correctly, she gave the impression that she'd never met Pendleton personally."

"Maybe she didn't." Brenda ran her fingers along the stem of her glass.

"It's possible, I suppose." I kept my tone even.

Now she looked up. "But you intend to find out?"

I didn't answer. I didn't have to.

Brenda sighed.

"Drink up," I said and drained my glass.

"Where are we going? To Antoinette's?"

"Not yet. I think I'll just look into this fishing business. Might want to try my luck." I signaled Clifford for a check.

Brenda set her mouth hard, then made her face go blank. I muttered, "Now, don't look at me like that . . ." I broke off as Clifford came up with the tab. I gave him a five-dollar bill and he went off to get change. Herbie and Jim, sitting at the bar, were sounding off on the high cost of living. "I can't help it, Brenda," I said. "I'm a cop."

She didn't answer. Clifford came back with my change. I thanked him and he assured us it had been a real pleasure to make our acquaintance.

Brenda came with me but slowly, silently. We walked along the sidewalk on Main Street past a variety store and a department store. I could see the gasoline emblem on a sign ahead of us. I tried once more to explain, "It's just that I've got to get to the truth of things. Just because Antoinette lied about knowing Pendleton . . ."

"She didn't lie. She didn't say she didn't know him. She didn't say that at all." Spoken vehemently. "And besides, he could have been here and she still didn't know him."

I looked askance at the thought. "She lied by omission, at least. The most natural thing in the world would have been for her to say, oh, he was in Vale awhile back . . . anyway, it doesn't necessarily mean anything. But surely you can understand, I just can't drop it, forget about it."

"It was a suicide. Tragic, but you of all people should know you can't stop a determined suicide. Why can't you accept that?" She stopped still on the pavement and two young men walking behind us had to back up and walk around. They looked at us curiously as they passed.

"I've tried to explain . . ." More people were approaching, this was one hell of a place to hold this discussion, right in the Middle of Main Street. "There's the Clements baby, for one thing, and Zelinda trying to break Pendleton's will and the way the man died . . . Jesus!" I could tell by her expression it was no use. "Go back to the inn if you want to. I've got to run this thing down and that's all there is to it."

Her jaw tightened. "No. I'm going with you."

I was good and mad now. The discussion had become an argument, pure and not so simple. "All right then," I growled. "Come on and shut up."

Henry Oliphant turned out to be a wizened little man in green coveralls who limped when he walked, squinted, too. He was pumping gas when we arrived at the station and he took his time about it. I walked inside the station with Brenda following. There was one chair behind a desk but neither of us sat in it. We stood, miles apart, and waited until the car at the pumps drove off. The little man made his way slowly into the office, wiping his hands on an oily rag. "What can I do for you folks?" he asked from the doorway. "Run out of gas?"

"I'm interested in fishing," I told him. My tone wasn't too cordial, I realized, so I added, "I hear you're the expert."

His face brightened. "I guess you could say it was my life's work." He gestured toward the pumps. "I just do this to earn a living." He grinned, his teeth looked to be false. "Want to go out tomorrow? I'm available."

I said carefully, "A fellow I knew said you know all there is to know about the fishing up here. Arthur Pendleton, remember him?"

He nodded, still smiling. "Sure. The guy who writes those heavy books." The grin faded. "He's dead, isn't he?"

I nodded. "A couple of months ago."

Oliphant shook his head in polite regret. Behind him a station wagon drove onto the apron, a bell rang inside the station. "Be right back," said Henry. He moved more quickly this time, almost double-timed his gimpy steps. Brenda remained silent, but I could feel her tenseness and I supposed she could sense my irritation. Damn it, she knew I was a cop when she married me.

"That Pendleton liked to fish and that's the truth," said Henry appearing again in the doorway with a credit card in his hand. He moved by me, to the desk with the card. "But he didn't do no fishing with me. Him and Tom Drew was fishing buddies. Tom durn near closed down his drugstore while Pendleton was in town. They was at the lake or on one of the streams most every day. Did you bring your gear with you? What are you aiming to go for, trout or salmon?"

"I haven't decided. We're visiting a relative, I don't know yet what her plans are for tomorrow. I guess I'd better check on it and get back to you."

"That so?" He put the credit card in its imprinting machine, ran it through. "Who are you visiting?"

"Antoinette Evers. My wife's cousin."

Henry peered at his charge slip to see if it was printed properly. "Went to school with Antoinette. Mighty fine woman." He looked up, faded blue eyes twinkling. "You tell her Henry'd be glad to guide you around any time. She'll be the judge."

"Thanks. I will." I waited until he'd quit the office bearing his charge form, then I followed him to the door. "Are you coming?" I asked Brenda.

"Oh, yes." Her voice was sharp. "To the drugstore, I presume?"

I didn't bother to reply. We walked, without speaking, back to the center of town, entered the drugstore across the street from the inn.

Tom Drew, it seemed, was a moon-faced man wearing dark-rimmed glasses and a white pharmacist's coat. He was waiting on a plump woman in a straw hat who couldn't make up her mind whether to buy Prell or White Rain shampoo. While we stood waiting for the crucial decision, Brenda fingered the perfumes arranged on the counter.

The plump lady at last opted for Prell, said, "Charge it, Tom," and went out with her package.

"May I help you?" Mr. Drew turned to us.

"I'd appreciate a few minutes of your time," I said pleasantly. "I'm doing some research on Arthur Glenn Pendleton and I understand you and he were friends."

Tom Drew blinked at me from behind his glasses, included Brenda in his glance. "Research?" he asked slowly.

I nodded without explanation.

"What kind of research?"

"My husband is a Boston detective," Brenda told him. "He's intent on investigating Mr. Pendleton's death."

I kept my face expressionless, which was quite a feat, considering.

"A detective." The druggist's face was as pokerlike as mine. "Yes, I read about Penn's unfortunate demise. Somebody said it was suicide."

"Is there a place where we could talk?" There were several people at the soda fountain where a girl in a white uniform was dispensing Cokes and ice cream. A man waited impatiently at the cigarette counter. I half expected Drew to say he was too busy but he didn't. "Just a minute," was what he said. "I'll get Mr. Turner's Marlboros and be right with you."

And it was just a minute, or little more, until he led us into the back room where prescriptions were compiled and where he offered us the use of two chairs beside a roll-top desk. He leaned against the desk itself and folded his arms. I scanned the shelves of powders and pills, asked, "Do you carry arsphenamine?"

The light was striking his glasses in a way so that I couldn't see his eyes. "No. No call for it. Never have used it in the twenty-some years I've been in the business." He motioned toward the desk. "You can check my records if you doubt me."

I didn't doubt him. From his very manner I knew I could study twenty years worth of drug orders and never find arsphenamine. But that didn't mean that he couldn't have gotten hold of it somewhere if someone asked him to . . . I looked at the desk top, noted the pipe rack, a stack of bills, a closed checkbook, a photograph of a woman and two little girls. "Your family?" I inquired.

"Yes."

"Pretty girls. How old are they?"

He changed positions and now I could see his eyes. They were wary. "Five and seven. It's a recent picture."

"When Pendleton was here in Vale, did he make out with any of the local talent?" I made my question deliberately crude. He was too cool, I wanted to shake him up.

119

"I wouldn't know about that. I went fishing with him. At night I went home to my family."

"How did you come to know him?" I wondered.

Drew shrugged. "He came to this part of the woods because somebody'd told him the fishing was great. He came in here to ask directions, we got to talking. I told him I did some fishing myself, he said could he come along. I said, why not? That's how it started. All I know about him is that he was a good companion. His personal life was his business."

And I knew that was all he intended to tell me. But I also knew that he might very well know the answer to my question. Yes, indeed. My vague instincts were beginning to make sense, at least to me. And I was damn sure that Antoinette Evers had been used in some way. It couldn't be just a coincidence that Pendleton had been in Vale "a couple of years ago" and that the Clements baby aged around fourteen months had been willed a million dollars. That baby's mother had to be here in Vale. I was certain of it.

"Mr. Drew . . ." The girl in the white uniform stuck her head in the door opening. "Mrs. Kennicutt wants a prescription."

I stood up. "Thank you very much," I said coldly. "Come along, Brenda. I'm hungry."

The desk clerk with the moustache had gone, was replaced by a young man wearing a seersucker suit. Brenda started up the stairs to the second floor and I said, "Where are you going?"

Without looking around, she answered, "To wash up before dinner. I'll be right down."

That was fine with me. "I'll wait here," I said. She didn't reply, disappeared from view.

I walked over to the desk. A small transistor radio was playing country music. "Nice evening," I remarked to the desk clerk.

"Great, isn't it? September's a good month, my favorite maybe. Not too hot, not too cold." He beamed, a professional smile.

"The foliage is beginning to turn. Must be quite a show when it's at its peak."

"Fantastic."

I leaned on the desk. "What's to do around here at night?"

"There's the movies . . . and a roadhouse out on the other side of town." He shrugged. "That's about all." His professional mask cracked as he added, "It's a pretty dull place in some ways."

"This your home town?"

He shook his head. "I'm a management trainee for Billington Inns, Inc. They run this place and I was assigned here two years ago." He sighed faintly. "About time to move on. I hope."

I used a casual tone, "You must have been here when the glamour boy was in town."

"The glamour boy?"

"Arthur Glenn Pendleton. The writer."

He looked blank. "Gee, I don't think so. I would have remembered . . ."

I had looked up my Zodiac. Those born under the sign of Leo were born between July 23 and August 22 and the Clements baby was born under the sign of Leo. "It would have been maybe October or November, year before last."

Light dawned. "That explains it. I didn't come here till just before Christmas. I must have just missed all the excitement. Biggest name I've seen around here was the lieutenant governor on a campaign tour."

I heard footsteps. Brenda was coming down. "So much for thrillsville," I said and went to meet her. We dined on roast duck and it was, as Clifford had said, first-rate.

I drove the car out of the parking lot up to the front door of the inn, reached over and opened the car door for Brenda. "Which way to Antoinette's?" I asked when she was in and settled.

"Turn right at the next corner." Her voice, in the darkness, sounded close to normal. I hoped she'd begun to realize that I had nothing against Cousin Antoinette, that I hadn't set out to make this scene in Vale. Subconsciously maybe, but not deliberately.

"Good dinner," I commented, turning right as she directed.

"Delicious. At the blinking light up ahead there, turn left."

"I wish I had the time to go fishing," I thought aloud.

"Some other time, perhaps." Her response was polite but not cold.

I peered at the street sign as I made the second turn. Oak Place. "Keep going," Brenda told me. "It's a few blocks more. Antoinette's house is on the edge of town."

Car lights from behind us shone in my rear-view mirror. I could see into houses as we drove along, people were eating, sitting, watching TV. Half a dozen shadowy forms in a front yard appeared to be youngsters busy at some before-bed game.

"Slow down now. It's up ahead, on the right. The small brown house with the split rail fence."

I obeyed Brenda's instructions and pulled up alongside the split rail fence. A glass-globed lamp shone softly at the front window. A yellow porch light illuminated a salmon-colored front door with a brass knocker. "I guess she's home," I said, opening my car door.

"It would seem so." Brenda's door clicked open.

There was a gate that creaked in an approved manner, and a flagstone walk. We went up the three steps, stood on the small porch and I lifted the brass knocker.

Almost immediately we heard footsteps coming near. The door opened and Antoinette, more childlike than ever in the partial shadow, looked out at us. "Brenda! Knute!" she exclaimed. "For goodness sakes, do come in. What a nice surprise!" And I looked at Brenda who wasn't looking at me. I had a strong hunch she'd telephoned Antoinette from the hotel while I was quizzing the room clerk.

Antoinette took us into the room with the globed light. It was a small room, the whole house was tiny, almost a doll's house. The gleaming furniture was properly scaled, even to a slender sofa with a rose-carved high back. I guessed that these were real antiques, not reproductions.

When had we arrived, how long could we stay, Antoinette wanted to know. I couldn't swear the questions were rehearsed but I was almost sure she already knew the answers. She took Brenda's hand, patted it. "Have you had supper?"

We had, I told her. She expressed disappointment. Brenda explained that we hadn't wanted to put her to any trouble. "Trouble?" she trilled. "My goodness, you're not putting me to any trouble."

There were pictures on the walls, old oils, ancestors, I gathered. There were framed photographs on the fireplace mantel. One was of a girl in a cap and gown, a graduation picture. I walked over and looked at it. "Doreen?" I asked, studying the wide dark eyes, the shy sweet smile.

"Yes." Antoinette was obviously proud. "Isn't she lovely?"

"She is." I put the picture back. "Where is she? Does she live with you?"

"She does when she's home. Her parents are gone, you see, I'm the only family. Right now she's at school. In

Burlington, at the university. She's made the Dean's List."

"Beauty and brains, huh?" I studied the other pictures. All family, obviously. Through the years. I spotted Doreen at various ages and I even found Brenda, a thin, awkward Brenda, but Brenda just the same in one of them.

"If only I'd known you were coming . . . the neighbors, the girls in my bridge club would love to meet you. And we could take a trip over the border, maybe you'd like to do that tomorrow. Have you ever been to Canada?" Antoinette was prattling on.

"We have to leave tomorrow," I told her, resuming my seat. "I only have two days off."

"Oh, dear." She wrinkled her small nose. "Well, at least tomorrow morning we could go out to the lake, take a lunch . . ."

"I think we'll have to leave pretty early," I apologized. "It's a long drive back to Boston."

"Why, that's almost no visit at all. Brenda," she patted Brenda's hand again, "can't you stay a few days with me? It seems such a shame to come way up here and go right back."

"Perhaps I could." Brenda looked me straight in the eye.

"If Knute wouldn't mind . . ." Antoinette gave me a pleading glance.

Putting me on the spot, were they? "I could drive back next week and pick her up," I told Antoinette. I didn't want Brenda to stay but damned if I'd beg her not to. If she'd only poke around for me, try and pick up some clue as to who the woman might be—but I knew without asking that she wouldn't. Unless I could convince her that finding out would let Antoinette off the hook. But it wouldn't exonerate Antoinette, I knew it wouldn't. Antoinette had to be a go-between, innocent or not.

"You could do something for me, Knute, on the way back," Antoinette was saying sweetly.

"Sure. What?"

"Drop off a package at the university for Doreen. It's her laundry and I'm a day late with it; if I mail it she won't get it until the first of the week."

"I'll be glad to." I meant it. I was most curious to meet Doreen Evers. She would have been seventeen two years ago, young, but not too young to have been dazzled by a famous writer, a worldly, older man. "What year is Doreen at college? Freshman?"

"Oh, no, she's a junior. She graduated from high school at sixteen." Antoinette put on that glowing look again.

A junior. Third year in college at nineteen. She could hardly have taken time out to have an illegitimate baby. Maybe Brenda was right. This thing was getting to be an obsession. I was looking under every cabbage leaf, no matter how small, for little bundles.

"I'll give you the box now so I won't forget it." Antoinette got up from the sofa, disappeared into the hall, reappeared, handed me a suit-box shape. A label on the

front of it read: Doreen Evers, care Mrs. Gwendolyn Torrey, Chapin Hall, University of Vermont. "Can I get you
something to drink?" Antoinette asked. "Or maybe coffee
and pound cake?"

"Have you got a beer?" I was suddenly thirsty.

"Oh, I'm afraid not." Antoinette looked abashed. "If
only I'd known . . ." She brightened. "I do have some
nice crème de menthe. I just love the color, don't you?"

"That will be fine," said Brenda with a glance that
warned me to silence.

And when we left, full of crème de menthe and carrying the laundry box, we had decided that I would bring
Brenda with suitcase back in the morning about nine.

At nine-thirty that next morning I paid a courtesy call
on the Vale police department.

As I drove alone through the Vermont hills, I mulled
over the next to nothing I'd actually learned.

The knowledge that Arthur Glenn Pendleton had been
in Vale at just about the right time had seemed to me
to be the break-through, the beginning of the windup.
Not so.

I mentally juggled my jigsaw pieces. I had a druggist
who could have, conceivably, supplied arsphenamine. I
had Antoinette who could have delivered it to Pendleton,
never mind the locked doors. I had a motive—the old
"done our girl wrong" bit, and an illegitimate baby.

And somewhere I had a vengeful mind, a mind that had devised an ugly and complicated scheme to do a man in.

Even if the murderer, and murderer he was in my opinion, wasn't sure the arsphenamine would kill, he'd taken pains to make sure he'd caused a goodly amount of mental anguish. He must have known Pendleton inside out, his aversion to doctors, his attitude toward his father who had taken his own life when he found he had syphilis. A carefully tailored plot fitted to one victim and only one victim, Arthur Glenn Pendleton.

But the good people of Vale, and good they seemed to be, had been nothing more than polite and kind. The police chief, one David Snider, appeared to be most cooperative. "Pendleton? He never got into any trouble in our town. Not even a traffic ticket. So you're married to Antoinette's cousin, huh? One of the best, Antoinette Evers. She's done a lot for the people in this town. Whenever somebody needs help, she's the first one they go to."

Furthermore, nobody knew anything about Pendleton and the fair sex. Not even the garrulous Clifford whom I'd visited again by going back into the bar before I went to bed. The best thing that had happened was that I'd had a beer to get rid of the crème de menthe taste.

I sighed and stretched my legs. I'd be coming back in a few days. There must be some sort of loose end in the complicated knot, I reasoned. I'd just have to keep looking for it.

I found Chapin Hall at the university with the help of a campus cop. I carted the laundry box into the dormitory lobby, asked a sweet young thing with eyes like saucers where I could find Doreen Evers.

She opened her eyes even wider. "Doreen Evers? Gee, I don't know her . . . are you sure she's in Chapin Hall?"

I showed her the laundry label. "Gee, I don't know, but then I don't know everybody. You'd better see Mrs. Torrey. She's in charge, she can tell you."

Mrs. Torrey had an office just off the main corridor. I knocked on her door. A trio of girls in blue jeans hurried by, giggling and lugging armloads of books. "Come in," said a voice from Mrs. Torrey's office. I obeyed.

Mrs. Torrey was an angular lady who sat tall and wore half-glasses down on the end of her nose. "I'm looking for Doreen Evers," I told her. "Her aunt sent her laundry." And I held out the box.

"I'll see that she gets it," said Mrs. Torrey, reaching for it.

"But couldn't I leave it with her myself? I have a message from her aunt."

Mrs. Torrey looked doubtful. "She's on a field trip."

"A field trip?"

"To New Hampshire. Geology. She's not due back until Monday."

"I see." I still hadn't let go of the box. "How is she doing? Feeling? That's what her aunt wants to know."

Mrs. Torrey pushed up her glasses and examined me

more thoroughly. "Tell Miss Evers that Doreen is absolutely fine. She is one of our brightest young ladies, shows great promise, we expect unusual things from her. Perhaps even a Rhodes scholarship."

"A girl?" I said without thinking.

Mrs. Torrey looked disdainful. "Perhaps," she said tartly, "you haven't heard of equal rights for women."

I gave up, handed Mrs. Torrey the laundry. "Tell her her aunt sent her love. Maybe I'll stop in to see her on my next trip."

"And when might that be?" asked Mrs. Torrey, cradling the laundry.

"Maybe next Thursday?"

"Oh, dear, I'm afraid that's her student teaching day."

"And where would she be student teaching?"

"That's hard to say. They rotate, you see."

"I see. Well, I'll catch up with her sometime. Thank you, Mrs. Torrey. For everything."

Her voice stopped me on my way out, "And what is your name?"

"Severson, Mrs. Torrey. Detective Knute Severson."

I have an acquaintance with the F.B.I., Milt Brannigan. I gave him a call on Monday morning and was lucky enough to find him in.

"I need a favor," I told him. "Scratch my back and I'll do the same for you one day."

"What's up?"

"Just an idea on something I'm playing with. To tell the truth, it's a way-out hunch. I'll give you a list of names and I'd like you to find out whatever you can about them. Like where they come from."

"Their addresses?"

"Home towns. Or maybe not home towns, but where they've lived. I've got a common denominator on my mind, but I could be out in left field. No harm done if I am, but no good either. It's just about my last loose end."

"You're being mysterious, Knute. Not to say obtuse. Anything we would be interested in?"

"I don't think so, but you never know. Mucho ramifications." Public health, adoption laws, maybe even interstate drug traffic. Or was it illegal to carry arsphenamine over state lines? I didn't know, in fact doubted it, but I needed Brannigan's interest.

"I'll do what I can. Give me your list."

I read off the names and present addresses. He whistled softly. "You do go far afield, don't you? This may take some time."

"How about Wednesday?" I asked. "Can do?"

"We'll see. I'll get back to you."

"Oh—Milt. There's one other thing. I'd like to nail down the whereabouts of one Doreen Evers. Got any ideas?"

"Is she missing? Has it been reported?"

"Not so far as I know. I'd just like to be sure she's where she's supposed to be."

"Why don't you go and find out?"

"I went, but I didn't find out."

"Has she got a social security number?"

"That I don't know."

"If she has, we can find her for you. If she had one, where would it have been issued?"

"Vermont. Vale, Vermont, I should think. And she's nineteen years old so it would have been in the last three years, if she has one."

"Well . . . nineteen, young. Maybe never paid taxes, either. But that narrows it down somewhat. What the devil are you up against, Knute?"

"Someone who thinks he's very clever."

"He?"

"Or she."

Brannigan laughed without amusement. "This modern world is on your side, boy. It gets tougher and tougher to be clever in these days of red tape and computation."

"I hope you're right, Milt." And after I'd hung up, I said it again. But then I wondered how Brenda would feel if and when I began to dig into the whole ball of wax.

When Brannigan hadn't called me back by Wednesday afternoon, I gave him a nudge. He was out, I was told, but due back in shortly. I left my number and name. "Tell him it's important."

Parks, at his desk next to mine, was doing the *Herald* crossword puzzle. It had been a slow day, in fact several slow days. Even the local colleges had been quiet this early week of a new session. I was pleased at the hiatus, but edgy just the same. I hadn't been able to find my favorite shirt that morning, couldn't tell whether Brenda had sent it to the laundry or had simply put it someplace where I couldn't find it. I was reminded of my mother telling my father, "George, if it had been a snake, it would have bitten you."

"When's Brenda due back, Knute?" Parks seemed to be reading my mind.

"I'm driving up tomorrow. We'll be back Friday." I didn't add, but thought, I hope.

"My wife wanted me to ask the two of you to come over to dinner one night." The kid was blushing again. The damnedest things embarrassed him. "How about next week?"

"I'll ask Brenda when I see her," I told him. Wendy Parks was, I thought, on the stupid side. I didn't think Brenda cared much for her company either, but the guy was my partner. Some sort of effort had to be made, I supposed. "I'm sure we can make it," I added.

"Good. She said Wednesday or Friday. You let me know. Either day's okay."

I nodded. The invitation made me wonder how Barbara and Benedict were doing in Florida. I hadn't heard from the son of a gun in over a month, he owed me a letter. Or did I owe him a letter? Brenda would know. . .

My phone rang. I picked it up and it was Brannigan. "Did you come up with anything?" I asked him.

"Some. Struck out once, on that Doreen Evers thing. She doesn't have a social security number, isn't on the tax rolls, so I couldn't find a handle there. I didn't dig around in her Vale, Vermont. I got the idea you didn't want us to."

"Okay. What about the others?"

"I was going to mail it to you . . ."

"I need it today."

"Got a pencil?"

"Yes. Shoot."

"Derek Pomfret, born Kalamazoo, Michigan, went to Los Angeles County with his parents in the late forties. Received his B.A. from University of Southern California, did graduate work at UCLA." Brannigan's information on Pomfret agreed with Pomfret's story. One down and four to go.

"G. Harding Fenster, born Omaha, Nebraska, studied at but did not graduate from the University of Omaha. Had a couple of brushes with the authorities when he was younger—a little old lady in Oklahoma brought him to court for plagiarism one time, no conviction. Traffic violations here and there, also a couple of drunken driving convictions. Now based in New York with the College of Creative Writing. Seems to be staying out of trouble in recent years."

I grunted but didn't count him completely out. "What about Antoinette Evers?"

"Let's see, Antoinette Evers. Born 1911 in Vale, Vermont, raised there. Graduated from Weston College for Women, 1931. Worked for the college for some twenty years following graduation, in the alumni department. Returned to Vale in the early fifties upon retirement from the college. Otherwise, no runs, no hits, no errors."

"Miss Cragmore?"

"Pamela Cragmore, born in Yonkers, is executive director of the Crib, a private adoption agency in New York City. Received degree in social work in 1938 from—Weston College for Women. Aha. That the connection you're looking for?"

I licked my lips. "Could be. Go on. Gwendolyn Torrey?"

"Maiden name Curtis. She's at the University of Vermont. Dormitory director, otherwise known as new-style house mother. Was born in Nashua, New Hampshire, received her teaching degree from—yep, the good old Weston College for Women."

"Well, well, well," I purred. "If I hurry I might just have time to run out to the Weston College for Women, seeing as how it's just a few miles away. Thanks, Brannigan. Remember, I owe you a favor."

"Got any Bruins' hockey tickets?"

"Are you kidding? I'm just a lowly detective. You can't get those things for love nor money."

"Well, I thought I'd try. I ask everybody. You never know."

Weston College for Women had gone coed, it seemed. Its tree-studded campus held mixed groups beneath myriad branches, at least I thought they were mixed. With the asexual trend in hair and clothes it was pretty hard to tell, but then I asked one downy-cheeked, blue-jeaned child the directions to the alumni office and he replied in a voice so bass he could sing "Asleep in the Deep."

The alumni secretary, a gone-to-seed and retired cheerleader type named Helen Constant, appeared startled when I introduced myself, but brightened when I mentioned Antoinette Evers. "Just a routine check," I lied glibly. "She's an incorporator in some sort of charity organization and we have to okay a certificate of character."

"What a relief." Miss Constant sighed, momentarily displacing a robust bosom. "We've gotten so uptight in recent years that the mere mention of the word police gives us palpitations. I mean, we instantly wonder what are they—meaning our little angels—up to now. Of course, I remember Miss Evers. She's not only my predecessor, but I was a student here while she was in this office. She was an unqualified darling."

"She left the college—what year?" Somehow I had to

get the names of Miss Cragmore and Mrs. Torrey into the conversation. Why couldn't they be incorporators too? Why not, indeed.

"Oh, dear, I'll have to look that up to be absolutely accurate. It must have been 1952 or 1953 . . ." She got out of her chair and trotted over to a filing cabinet. She still had good legs. "No, I was a year off. It was in 1951." She came back, bearing a manila folder. "She left that summer. The reason I guessed wrong is because I didn't come until early '54. They had an acting secretary in between."

"Did Miss Evers give any reason for leaving?"

"Let me see." She referred to the folder. "Early retirement. She'd been here since 1932, almost twenty years. She was only forty years old and the pension plan then wasn't what it is now, but I guess she'd had enough. Besides, I'm sure there was money in the family. Her father was a doctor, you know."

A doctor. Well, well. Nobody'd bothered to mention that small fact. I pretended to consult my notebook. "Pamela Cragmore. She's another incorporator. When did she graduate from Weston?"

"Pam? For goodness sakes, isn't that interesting. Now, whatever can those girls be getting into? I don't suppose you'll tell me, but I'll bet it's something worthwhile. Wait a second, I'll have to check on that, too. The memory fades inversely in direct proportion to the years, you know." She twinkled at me, went to another file. "1938, Pam was a member of the class of 1938. I knew her because she and Antoinette were pals. When she was working in Boston, she often came out to the campus."

"And Gwendolyn Torrey? Gwendolyn Curtis, she would have been then."

"Oh, she was a year or two ahead of me." She manipulated more folders. "What do you know, I was wrong. 1946. She was a year behind me."

"Then perhaps she and Miss Evers weren't as close as Miss Evers and Miss Cragmore?"

"Oh, they were friends all right, despite the age difference. Gwen taught here for a couple of years, she majored in education."

"They must have kept in touch all through the years." In close touch, so close that one could be called upon at any time for any sort of favor. Privileged information. Or a lie.

"Oh, I should imagine so. Antoinette is a compulsive letter writer. And she has such a warm way about her. I still get letters from alumni asking how she is after all this time. She made a lasting impression."

I sighed and closed my notebook. Pieces were dovetailing, creating a shape in the shadows. My emotions were mixed. Gratification—and—what? Disappointment? A sense of betrayal? Or did I feel some sort of strange apprehension? As though I were walking too easily into

some strange scene that appeared to be woods on a clearly
marked trail that might turn to quicksand? When I least
expected it?

I didn't bother to stop in Burlington on my way back.
Old school buddy Gwendolyn Torrey no doubt had her
story all set. Geology trip last time, student teaching this
time and if I tried again, Miss Doreen Evers would no
doubt still be incommunicado. I don't know how I knew,
but I was sure as hell the girl wasn't there. The Torrey
woman's excuses were just too glib. Yet, if she wasn't,
where was she? And how was I going to find out?

Even if I knocked on doors in every street in Vale,
my instincts told me that no one would say. A nice
little closed corporation—hadn't been too far wrong,
either, in saying that Antoinette was an incorporator.

Clifford had sent me winging when he told me Pendleton had been there. Either he was too stupid to know
what that meant or too innocent. Probably both. Maybe
I should just come right out and pin Antoinette to the
wall with the direct question? Several direct questions.

Brenda would have a fit.

But if I could find Doreen, talk to her . . . maybe
I *was* all wet. At seventeen would Pendleton have appealed to her, or she to Pendleton? He had been attracted
to June Carr who was definitely young—and sexy. Could

be Doreen was a Lolita type. Not that her pictures showed it.

On the other hand, could be that what I suspected couldn't possibly be. But I wanted to know, damn it. I had to know.

If—and I was jumping to conclusions like a steeple-chaser—if Pendleton had fathered the Clements baby and the mother was Doreen Evers, Antoinette could have arranged for the adoption through another Weston alumna, Pamela Cragmore. And, having done that, Antoinette could have told Pendleton who had adopted the baby.

But why?

So the baby would be provided for.

But wasn't she taking a chance that Pendleton might try to get the child himself?

What gave me the idea he might want the child? Something June Carr had said—he'd always wanted a son.

Then, why didn't he simply marry the mother and give the child his name, his birthright? If they weren't compatible, Pendleton and the mother, they could have gotten a divorce. I couldn't answer those questions, I simply didn't know that much about the man. Or the woman.

Wait . . . I'd forgotten the venereal disease ploy. If somehow he'd been convinced that he had the thing . . . how had he been convinced? Was the mother infected?

Extremely doubtful, since he hadn't contacted the disease after all.

Damn. I stepped on the accelerator. I had to find Doreen Evers.

I slowed down. But how?

Who in Vale could I go to with any hope of an answer?

I took a curve too fast, had to brake. The nosy postmistress. Antoinette's only slighting reference to anybody in her home town.

And who would have more diversified information than a nosy postmistress?

Now I accelerated and kept my speed steady. Good thing I'd left early. I could get there before the post office closed.

The desk clerk with the moustache was on duty, recognized me when I came in. "Mr. Severson, isn't it?"

"That's right. Got a room for me?"

"Of course, and I have a message for you, too."

It was a note from Brenda. It said: "Dear Knute, I called you yesterday and this morning, but couldn't reach you either time. I don't know just when you'll arrive, but if you do check into the inn first I want you to know that Antoinette has planned a party for you this evening. She's invited all her friends to meet you and the party starts at seven. Please, Knute, don't disappoint her. And,

Knute, she says to tell you that Doreen thanks you for delivering the laundry box."

I put the note in my pocket, reread it again in the room. Don't disappoint her! That was like a mother telling her son to be a good boy and mind his manners. And Doreen thanks you. Cute. Very cute. I hung up my clothes hurriedly and walked across the street to the post office.

It was a small post office built of granite. There were three spaces for customers, an in-town mail slot and an out-of town mail slot and a wall of postal boxes. Alongside these on a bulletin board hung the usual wanted posters.

The three spaces for customers were filled when I came in. One woman was sending a money order with the help of a pimply-faced young man. Another woman was filing a custom's declaration for her parcel with the help of a thin-faced woman with curly red hair. A man was ordering stamps for his stamp collection from a portly gentleman wearing a gray button-front sweater. I got in line behind the customs declaring lady.

When her business was finished, I took her place. "Are you the postmistress here?" I asked in official tones.

The thin face lengthened. "I am. Mrs. Gilmanton, postmistress. What can I do for you?"

I flashed my identification. "I'd like to talk to you." I put my wallet back. I wasn't sure she'd spotted the

Boston address and I didn't intend to explain that unless I had to.

"Yes, of course." Her nose twitched like a rabbit's. "Come into my office, Mr.—?"

"Severson. Detective Severson." I'd kept my voice low, but I could feel the man and the youth looking at me, then glancing away.

I passed through a doorway by the mail slots, sat across from Mrs. Gilmanton's desk. Her nose twitched once more and she rubbed at it. "What can I do for you?"

"I'm looking for some information on the mailing habits of one of the citizens of Vale," I told her gruffly.

She looked down at her desk top but not before I saw the sparkle in her close-set eyes. "Who are you investigating?"

"A Miss Antoinette Evers."

She fluttered her eyelashes and this time I saw the spark catch fire. "Antoinette? Miss Evers? Whatever for? She is one of our most respected residents."

"I'm not at liberty to tell you the reason." I was bluffing and I hoped I was bluffing well.

"She does a great deal of mailing, of course . . ." Mrs. Gilmanton picked up an ink pad and a rubber stamp, began to play with them like a toy. "She says they are manuscripts." She looked up at me. "Gets a special rate."

"I know about that," I told her. I put all the hidden meaning that I could into the sentence.

"You mean—they aren't manuscripts? It's something else . . ." She leaned closer, dropped her voice. "Something illegal?"

I stared back without comment.

"And she's so uppity," said Mrs. Gilmanton, almost talking to herself. "Having a party tonight for half the town she is, and do you think she'd . . ." She broke off. "What do you want to know about Miss Evers' mail?"

"Who she writes to. Where letters come from. Not all, of course. But the frequent ones. Constant correspondence."

"Oh, dear." She nibbled at her thin lower lip. "Well, I'm not sure I could find that out without paying close attention. I mean, I naturally don't look to see . . ." We watched each other.

I said, very quietly, "It's a matter of extreme urgency."

She drew in her breath. "I have noticed a couple of addresses . . . I mean, she writes there so often and one can't help but notice . . ."

I nodded, produced my notebook and pen.

"One place is the Canadian National in Montreal. I don't know just what the Canadian National is . . ." She gulped. "Could she have anything to do with all that unrest in Canada lately? I mean, those subversive people?"

I tried to seem to be trying to seem noncommittal. If I remembered correctly, the *Canadian National* was a periodical of some sort. "Who else?"

She frowned, trying to remember. "Some place in New

York—oh, yes. Something called a Creative School of Writing. She says she's a writer, you know."

"We know."

"And to some school in Massachusetts. Weston College, I think it is. And to people all over the country, only she doesn't do that as often. Her postage bills are large, though, I can tell you. Still not as large as they should be if she weren't getting a manuscript rate."

"To anyone in Vermont?"

"She used to write to her niece at the university. But she hasn't been doing that of late. Oh, and there's a recent one. A woman in Boston. Singleton or some such name. Begins with an S."

That accounted for Brenda's letters. Mrs. Gilmanton didn't pay much attention to Antoinette's mail—not much!

"But no one in Vermont?" Probably Doreen was far away. Perhaps she'd taken another name, but why would she do that? Unless everyone in town knew about the baby. That sort of grand conspiracy was too hard to swallow. It couldn't be—for one thing, if everyone knew, Mrs. Gilmanton would be sure to tell me.

"Vermont? No, I don't think so—bills, that sort of thing, the phone company and tax bills and hospital bills. . . ."

I jumped on it. "Hospital bills?"

"Why, yes. Our closest hospital is in Hickey, that's about twenty-five miles away. I've noticed she's been sending them checks regularly, at least I suppose they're checks. Probably paying for that illness she had last year on the installment plan." She sniffed.

Twenty-five miles away. Pay dirt? I reached over and put my hand on top of Mrs. Gilmanton's. Her hand trembled. "I must ask you to remain very quiet about this. As I said before, it's a vital matter."

Her mouth opened, closed, opened again. "Yes, yes, of course. Is it something about the hospital . . . ?"

I raised my eyebrows and shook my head, closed my notebook, gave another warning nod and got out of there.

It took me twenty minutes to get to Hickey. I pulled up in front of a policeman on traffic duty in the square and called to him, "Where's the hospital?" It was almost six o'clock. I wanted to get there before the business offices closed.

A car honked behind me and behind that one, another. "What'd you say?" asked the officer.

I shouted, "Where's the hospital?"

Several cars honked. Just because I was holding up traffic on the main thoroughfare at peak traffic time. The cop said something that I couldn't hear through the cacophony of sound.

"What did you say?" I yelled.

He sighed, came right over to my window and leaned in. "I said," he said patiently, "which hospital do you want? The regular hospital or the mental hospital?"

"Jesus Christ!" I said involuntarily. "The mental hospital. I guess I want the mental hospital."

"Go to the third set of lights, turn right, go straight ahead, it's on top of the hill." He moved away from the car, horns honked and he leaned over once more. "And get the hell out of here."

"Thank you for seeing me, Dr. Franklin," I said. "I'm married to Doreen Evers' cousin and we'd like to know how she's coming along."

And Dr. Franklin, perfectly cast for the part of eminent psychologist with his handsome head of waving white hair and steel-blue eyes, answered, "We believe we are making progress, Mr. . . . ?"

"Severson. Knute Severson."

"Mr. Severson. Of course, these things take time but I have great hopes for Doreen . . ." He smiled, almost boyishly. "We doctors are supposed to be objective about these things, but she is such a lovely child that it's all I can do to keep from being personally involved. You can believe me when I say that the entire staff gives her special attention."

Now or never. I had to make some very accurate stabs in the dark. "Is she still so . . . ?" I groped for the right word.

"Depressed? Some days, yes. But of late, we have been able to make temporary break-throughs, establish some meaningful communication. . . ."

"I don't suppose I could see her? Just for a moment?

I don't know what your visiting rules are, but I was up this way this afternoon and my wife has been so concerned . . ."

He pursed well-shaped pink lips. "It's getting on to dinnertime. We have our routine, you know. Our patients seem to feel more secure with a definite schedule, not that we're rigid about it . . . that wouldn't do either."

"If I could just see her for a few minutes." I tried to give a man-to-man grin. "I'm not sure what my wife will say to me if I go back and tell her I didn't see Doreen." I held up a package I'd hurriedly bought at Drew's drugstore in Vale. A gift for the patient, if there was a patient, had been my plan. If not, a peace offering to Brenda. "Perfume," I explained. "My wife picked it out. It's called Crêpe de Chine."

"Well . . ." Dr. Franklin smiled. His teeth were perfect, in keeping with the whole. "I don't see why not. For—let's say, fifteen minutes." He picked up a telephone, pushed a button. "Kimball, would you bring Miss Evers down to the visiting room right away? Thank you." He hung up, looked suddenly somber. "If this is one of her more troubled days, please don't be distressed. I assure you she has good days as well."

"I understand." If my voice quivered slightly with emotion, that was all right, too. He didn't know which emotion caused the quiver. But then, neither did I. Not exactly.

The visiting room of Hickey Sanitarium was large,

bright and currently empty. From what I could see, it looked to be a good hospital. Expensive. If Antoinette was paying the bills, and it seemed she was, no wonder she had financial problems.

I walked over to a window and looked out. It was twilight, the last glows of the sun gave a gold-red rim to the horizon. Vermont's green mountains looked purple. As I stood there, enjoying the view, I sensed someone behind me. I turned quickly around.

She stood just inside the doorway, almost huddling against it, hands clasped tightly in front of her.

I thought that she was beautiful, that there was no other word to describe her and then I looked into her wide, dark eyes and thought she wasn't beautiful at all.

Her hair was a red-gold glory, falling about her shoulders. She wore a long, pink dress, the sort that girls wear now in the daytime, the skirt was full, fell gracefully from a small waist. All my doubts as to whether she would have appealed to Pendleton vanished. Except for what I saw in her eyes, she would have appealed to any man alive.

"Doreen," I said tentatively, "I'm Brenda's husband, your cousin Brenda."

She didn't answer. Her eyes widened like a startled animal's, but she didn't move or change position.

I took a step forward. "How are you?" I held out the package. "Brenda sent you this."

The only response was another change in the eyes.

I took two steps this time. "We're staying with Antoinette. We live in Boston. We haven't been married very long, that's why you and I haven't met before. My name's Severson. Knute Severson."

"I don't remember any Brenda." Her voice was a clear contralto, pleasant to hear.

"Brenda Purdue. From New Hampshire. Only she's Brenda Severson now." Half a dozen steps, taken easily without haste. Somehow it was like approaching a small wild thing in the forest.

"What color is her hair?" Her pose had stiffened, she was not so much huddling now as poised—to run?

"Dark brown. Almost black. And her eyes are dark, too, like yours. She's very pretty, my wife, Brenda."

"I think I remember someone like that." All at once the stiffness left her and she came forward in one fluid movement, the skirt billowing softly around her ankles. "What's in the package? Is it for me?"

"Yes." I held it out. "It's for you."

She reached and took it from me, but she didn't open it. She used her eyes, almost like feelers, to examine my face. "What do you want from me?" she asked. Her voice was far away.

"Nothing. Just to talk. Why don't we sit down?" I indicated a comfortable-looking sofa.

"Over there." She pointed, it was an order. "You sit over there." Over there was an armchair. I sat in it. She sat on the sofa with the package in her lap.

"Why don't you open it?" I asked.

She ignored my question. "I know who you are." She spoke in a high, taut tone. "You took him. You're the one who took him."

"Took him? I didn't take anyone. I'm Brenda's husband."

She looked blank. "What are you talking about?"

"You said I took—your baby." I grabbed that out of thin air. "But I didn't. Truly I didn't."

She sat straighter, put on a haughty expression, "I don't know what you're talking about. I don't understand you at all." And then, "You're lying. You took him."

I tried a different tack. "How long have you been here, Doreen?"

She looked around. "Where am I?"

"In the hospital. You've been ill for how long? Over a year?"

She began to tear at the edges of the paper that was wrapped around the perfume. "I've always been here," she said petulantly.

I thought about what to say next. God knew, I didn't want to harm her, to add to her confusion. "Did you know that Arthur Pendleton is dead?" I spoke the words gently.

She laughed. I couldn't tell whether she laughed at my question or at the Crêpe de Chine bottle which she'd unwrapped. "He died over two months ago," I told her.

She looked up. The wildness in her eyes had been preempted by mirth, mirth that made them sparkle, that let me know how her eyes must have looked before her sickness. "Who?" she asked with an unsmiling mouth while her eyes danced.

"Arthur Glenn Pendleton." Very softly said.

She screamed, only once, a very high scream, very thin, and threw the perfume bottle at me. It smashed against the wall and the room was filled with a sweet, sweet odor.

Someone came running. It was a male nurse, a young man with a pock-marked face wearing a white jacket and pants. He stopped at the doorway, looked in. No one spoke to him, Doreen was sitting quietly on the sofa. "Everything all right?" he asked.

Doreen shook her hair as though to clear her head, got up from the sofa and stretched tall. It was a sight to see, I watched the nurse watching her. Then she turned, almost dancing, and went up to him. "He tried to rape me," she said sweetly and threw her arms around him, plastered her body against him.

I stood up, started to protest her statement, but he reached up calmly, removed her clutching arms, stepped away from her. "Now, Doreen," his voice was patient, matter-of-fact, but he was breathing hard. "You know he didn't. He was clear across the room from you."

"Well, he wanted to." She pouted like a spoiled child.

"We're cousins," I said lamely. "By marriage. I wouldn't . . . I didn't . . ."

"Why don't you be a good girl now and run along to dinner." The male nurse looked down into her face, gave her arm a gentle pat. "I think it's baked chicken. You like that, don't you? Baked chicken with mashed potatoes?"

"And stuffing? And cranberry sauce?" She smiled up at him, enchanting.

"I think so. Why don't you go see?"

She turned to me, curtseyed like a small girl at dancing school. "Nice to have met you, Mr.—Seman, is it? Any friend of my father and mother's is a friend of mine." And she dimpled at me, whirled and ran down the hall, holding her skirts, transformed from a child at dancing class to a bride at her reception.

"I . . ." my voice sounded strange, I cleared my throat, started again. "I hope I didn't upset her. I didn't intend to."

"I don't think you did. That rape business—it's one of her aberrations. She's afraid of men, at least a part of her is." He looked embarrassed. "She's come to trust me."

"I mentioned the baby. Maybe I shouldn't have."

"She talks about it sometimes. She's beginning to accept the situation." He started to say something else, changed his mind. Perhaps he'd thought he'd said too much.

I showed him the perfume stain on the wall. "I'm afraid my gift caused a cleanup problem."

"We'll take care of it. Shall I show you out, Mr.— I didn't get the name."

"Severson. And you're . . . ?"

"Kimball. Francis Kimball." We shook hands awkwardly. I wanted in the worst way to put more questions to him, only I hadn't any idea how he'd react. What the hell, I'd been grasping at straws from Boston to Vale. I started down the hall with him, said, "Does she talk about the baby's father?"

He gave me a quick glance, I kept my face open, curious, a close-relative face. "Not to me," he said after a moment. "If she talks about anything to me, I just talk around it and report it. I'm no doctor, just a glorified baby sitter."

"You were good with her just now," I told him. There had been no bitterness in his tone, but there had been a kind of sorrow.

"I like her. I like a lot of them. I wish I knew much more . . . how to really help . . ." his voice trailed off and he laughed. "That's what I get for not liking school," he said ruefully. "I barely made it through high school, let alone medical school. Well, here's the exit, Mr. Severson. And don't you feel bad about what she said in there. She doesn't mean it, honest she doesn't. She says that about most everybody."

"Thanks. And take good care of her, will you?"

"Kimball?" A female nurse appeared at the other end of the hall, beckoned. I watched him walk away, an earnest, slightly stooped young man in a starched white suit. Little did he know that we had something in common—we both worked at helping people. Only, right now I preferred his methods—and his motives.

The street in front of Antoinette's house was lined with cars so I had to park some distance away and walk.

As I came up the walk I could see that the wooden front door was open and through the glass of the storm door I spied several people standing in the hallway outside the living room, evidently a spillover of too many bodies in too small a space. I opened the storm door and walked in.

Those in the hall looked at me in a friendly manner. I nodded to them, excused myself, walked through them to the archway. Antoinette, clad in a bright blue silk dress, was talking animatedly to a group of ladies. Brenda stood beside her and it was she who spotted me in the entrance. "Here's Knute," she told Antoinette. Antoinette broke off her conversation to come forward, edging her way past people.

"Ladies and gentlemen," she caroled, "here's our guest of honor. Brenda's husband, Knute. Come and meet everyone, my dear."

"Good evening," I said over and over again and only half-heard the names she spoke, there were so many of them.

Brenda walked alongside me, asked, "When did you get here? I called this morning but you must have left before nine."

"Late this afternoon," I told her. "How do you do?" I acknowledged another introduction.

Antoinette's friend Harley reminded me that we'd met before. "Of course we have," I said much too heartily, embarrassed that I'd forgotten him.

"I remember Brenda from the days when she had braces on her teeth," one silver-haired lady told me. "She spent so many of her summers here in Vale."

I smiled, said the only thing I thought appropriate, "Vale's a fine town. Brenda has many fond memories of it."

"Antoinette tells us you're a police officer," this from a male contemporary of my hostess.

"Yes, I'm a detective in Boston." We were progressing slowly, nearing the dining room where more guests were ringed around a table laden with a huge punch bowl and platters of food.

The outside door opened and someone else came in. I couldn't see too well from where I stood but it looked to be Drew, the druggist. I estimated that there were, perhaps, fifty people in the house, nearly all of whom remembered Brenda from her summers in Vale, who had heard that I was a policeman and who felt bound to tell me what a fine woman Antoinette Evers was.

It was getting warm, my shirt felt damp under my

jacket. I managed to gulp a turkey sandwich and I was thirsty, wondered what was in the punch bowl. "Have some mulled cider, Knute," Antoinette urged. She seemed to be in her element, eyes shining, face alive. She looked considerably younger in the gleam of candles and soft lights.

"Cider?" I looked suspiciously into the cup somebody put into my hand.

"Hard cider," Brenda spoke from behind me. "It's closely related to apple jack."

"Harley's wife makes it in her kitchen," somebody else said. "He's got a couple dozen fine apple trees on his place. Best mulled cider I ever tasted."

"Antoinette . . ." a female voice spoke from the other side of the table, she was a young matron type with short dark hair; a bulging waistline told me she was about to become a mother. "How is Doreen? I haven't seen her in ages. Didn't she come home this summer?"

I thought, but wasn't sure, that there was a sudden silence. But if there was one, it was brief. "She's doing awfully well, Lydia," Antoinette answered with enthusiasm. "And she didn't come home this summer because she went to France on one of those student exchange programs. She had a wonderful time!"

"The opportunities kids get nowadays," sighed a man to my right.

"All the chances in the world," said somebody else.

"If only they'll take them," another added. "Did you

hear about Ned Cole's boy? Got himself arrested in some drug raid. . . ." I downed my cup of cider. It was pretty good. I had another.

The crowd finally began to leave around eleven, but it took them close to an hour to clear out. They departed in groups of twos and fours, each pausing to deliver good wishes to Brenda and me and thanking Antoinette for "a lovely party. But then, you always give a lovely party."

"If you got here this afternoon," said Brenda in low tones to me, "why were you so late getting over here?"

"I had a few things to do. Nice to have met you, Mr. Tobin, Mrs. Tobin. If you're ever down Boston way . . .'"

As the last of the visitors were saying their good-bys, I ducked back into the dining room where there was maybe a couple of inches of mulled cider left in the bowl. I scooped out another cup for myself, downed it. Antoinette and Brenda found me there staring into my empty punch cup.

"I just love parties," Antoinette said happily. "I'm grateful to you and Brenda for giving me an excuse for one. I haven't entertained in ages."

"Antoinette . . ." Brenda's voice was wary. I waited for her to finish her sentence, but she didn't.

"Is something wrong?" Antoinette spoke slowly.

I put the cup down on the littered table, turned to look at her. "I visited Doreen this afternoon." I watched her face.

She smiled, very widely, very brightly. "How nice. She

must have been glad to see you. I've told her all about you, how kind to me you were in Boston."

"I don't think she knew who I was."

The smile might have been painted on. "Did she say when she was coming home? Perhaps not until Thanksgiving or Christmas . . . She's so busy . . . so much to learn at school . . . so many friends keeping her occupied . . ." Her voice trailed off, something happened to her eyes, but that awful smile remained.

"Let's sit down," I suggested, "and talk."

"I've got to clear the table." Antoinette's hands began to stack plates on plates, a fork, then a spoon fell to the floor, she wasn't looking at what she was doing, she was smiling at me . . .

I took her arm. "Let's sit down."

I walked her into the living room, sat her on the rose-carved sofa. Brenda sat beside her, I sat across from them. I had a headache. Heat, no doubt, too many people and too much mulled cider.

"You don't need to pretend any more," I told Antoinette. "I know all about it, or almost all. You can fill me in when I go wrong."

Brenda whispered something. I thought it was "Damn you."

"Around two years ago Arthur Glenn Pendleton came up to Vale to do some fishing. Why he picked this place —who knows? He was a sportsman, enjoyed out-of-the-way unspoiled places. Maybe he came because of something you wrote, Antoinette, I don't know. I only know he came and he came across Doreen Evers. As you said, an extremely lovely young lady."

Antoinette watched me in fascination, mouth slightly open. Her eyes gleamed so, I couldn't make out the expression behind the gleam.

"Doreen was young and lovely and most impressionable. When he began to pay attention to her, she responded. Responded so thoroughly that when Pendleton left, she was carrying his baby. Here's where you come in—what you did when you found out, I can only imagine. Wrote him, I suppose. Did you insist that he marry her and he refused? You'll have to answer that."

Antoinette's head turned, almost like an owl's, it moved so slowly, her eyes were so still. "Knute should write," she told Brenda. "He has a marvelous imagination. What they call a storytelling sense."

Brenda didn't answer, only reached for Antoinette's hand.

"Anyway, the baby was born a year ago August. And when the baby was born, Doreen lost control. It was too much for her, an illegitimate child and one born with a birth defect, too, then taken from her and given to someone else. She cracked, literally, and you sent her to Hickey Sanitarium for psychiatric help."

Brenda must have been holding her breath. She released it now, slowly.

"But you made sure that no one knew. That is, almost

no one. You rallied your friends—Mrs. Torrey at the university, for instance. She would lie for you if anyone from Vale got too curious. And you had Miss Cragmore to handle the adoption of the baby. Everything very neat . . . I don't know where you took Doreen to have the baby, but I suspect that was easy for you as well. A different name, a different town, a made-up story. That doesn't interest me so much right at the moment. But what you did to Pendleton at this point does interest me. You let him know that the child had been adopted, you let him know who adopted him, and you convinced Pendleton that he was dangerously ill. From his viewpoint, perhaps incurably ill."

I paused so that she could tell me how or why she did it, but she didn't say a word. Her mouth tried to stretch back into its smile, didn't quite make it. So I went on.

"Your father was a doctor. You got the arsphenamine either from his old medical supplies, or from another doctor, an old friend, you're great at utilizing friends. Maybe even Tom Drew got hold of it for you, that's not important. You took it with you to Boston, what a heaven-sent opportunity, that writers' convention. Coincidental? I guess, but where and when didn't matter. You would have gotten to Pendleton sooner or later, no matter where he was. You only had to wait and you'd already driven him half crazy with your newsy letters from Vale."

"Even if this is all true . . ." Brenda's tone was tight,

"how did she make him use the stuff? How did she get it to him?"

"You said I had imagination, Antoinette. I'll use it now. I'm Arthur Glenn Pendleton, see, and I'm air sick in my Boston hotel room, more than air sick, actually, because some woman has convinced me that I have VD just like my father before me, and I've decided to kill myself. So I'm lying there, damned miserable, terrified. Waiting.

"Then my secretary calls on the phone and says that Antoinette Evers is there to see me. It is Antoinette Evers I've been waiting for, but I'm afraid of her. I recognize her—she is death and this place isn't Boston at all, it's a city called Samarkand. I panic, I say don't let her in whatever you do. Lock the doors, tell her to go away. And I lie there, sweating. I know that vengeance is waiting outside that door. Every debt I've ever owed has come due and the collector is sitting out there. Maybe I even go to the bathroom to throw up after I've locked my connecting door. I hear Pomfret lock the other door and I lie there. Life is hopeless now. I'm like my father. Except that my father had a son—only I have a son, too, but he isn't with me, I can't have him. I can't enjoy him, I can't enjoy teaching him, I can't enjoy writing or loving or living . . ."

Now it was Brenda who stared at me as though bewitched.

"So I'm Arthur Glenn Pendleton and I'm lying there . . . and I wait until I'm sure Pomfret has gone, then I

crawl up from my bed and open the connecting door for
her. 'Did you bring it?' I ask. 'Did you bring it?'

"Oh, yes, she's brought it, she said she would when I
asked her to find it for me. And I am not surprised, I
knew all the time she wanted me dead. She reaches out
with the needle and the arsphenamine, puts it in my
hand. I stare at it, fascinated. Do I have the courage after
all? Death is so final. One more chance? Shouldn't I
have one more chance? Didn't God mean for everyone
to have just one more . . ."

I was living it now. I'd thought so much about how it
must have been that I was Arthur Glenn Pendleton in
that moment. "Then she says something, I'll have to guess
what it was. I think the right words then might have
saved him, but she says something like, 'It's easy. I'll do
it if you like.' 'No!' I almost scream. 'No, I'll do it myself!' 'All right,' she says, 'have it your own way.'

" 'Get out,' I say, 'leave me alone.' I touch the sharp
tip of the needle, hardly hearing her go. I know how to
do it. You just fill the needle by pulling out the plunger,
you inject it in the arm by pushing the plunger in. And
I gag at the thought but I know I must do it. Quickly I
lock the door again.

"Back in my bed, I look at the hypodermic and the
medicine with aversion. I believe it's my only way out,
my fate, and yet it takes minutes, many minutes before
I can bring myself to try it. The needle gleams, its point
is too sharp, it will hurt, I am inexperienced, I don't do

it well, but at last I do it and lay back, wondering how it feels to die, to actually die, thinking I should write it down (he would think that, I think) and what happens is that he begins to feel very strange and then very sick, sick in a way he has never felt sick before and then . . ."

"Remarkable," said Antoinette to Brenda.

I found a handkerchief in my pocket and wiped my brow. I felt exhausted.

"Tell him it isn't true," Brenda urged Antoinette.

Antoinette smiled, a new, curiously gentle smile. "Remarkable," she said again. "This is an unusual young man you've married, Brenda."

Brenda stood up. "Well, if you won't protect yourself, I'll have to do it for you." She spoke coldly. "I'm going to call Mr. Greathead, get him up here right away."

I opened my mouth, shut it. If that's the way she wanted it, she could have her esteemed lawyer Greathead. She stared at me a moment, I glared back. When she turned and went out of the room, I went after her but while she turned toward the kitchen, I walked out the front door.

I spent a most unpleasant night at the Vale Inn.

Charles Evans Greathead came into Antoinette's house like a Roman emperor. His mane of silver hair had grown longer, curled now at the edge of his boldly striped shirt collar. Brenda went up to him and I glanced away.

I should have begged her to leave him out of it. But I wouldn't. I couldn't.

"Thank you, Charles," Brenda murmured, "I know how busy you are."

"Never too busy for you, you know that. Here's the bridegroom. How are you, Knute?"

He put out his hand and I shook it. What else could I do? But all I said was "Fine, thanks." And curtly.

"This is Cousin Antoinette Evers." Brenda led him over to the sofa where Antoinette sat a la Queen Victoria. A wild scene, I thought, a Roman emperor and Queen Victoria.

"How do you do, ma'am." He made a courtly gesture straight out of the old Clarence Darrow-inspired movies.

"You look expensive, Mr. Greathead." Antoinette raised her little chin. "I haven't got much money."

He settled himself in the armchair across from her, my armchair. "Don't let that bother you," he said expansively. "You can call this a labor of love."

Damn the man!

He leaned back, removed a gold case from his pocket, took his time about removing and lighting a cigar. He'd arrived in style that morning in a Lear jet that had landed on the Vale High School football field. How arrogant could you get?

Greathead looked around for an ash tray and Brenda brought him one. "Now." He did the whole bit, smoke ring blowing and all. "Let's start from the beginning."

"You made the trip for nothing," I told him.

He glanced my way, but otherwise ignored me. Brenda began to talk, Antoinette looking on like an interested bystander. "Knute has accused Antoinette of supplying Arthur Glenn Pendleton with the drug that killed him," she put it succinctly. "I don't know if he plans to charge her with murder, manslaughter, being an accessory before or after the fact or just what."

Greathead blew another smoke ring. "Interesting case," he said. "I looked into it a bit further after you called last night. But I should imagine the district attorney wouldn't care much for it."

"Of course he wouldn't," I said scornfully. "They didn't let me finish my speech last night. Even if I got Antoinette to agree to come back, or took out extradition papers, we'd never get a conviction. Suppose she confessed? How could we prove intent? Sentence her because she brought him a dosage that might—or might not—kill him? We'd have our jails filled if we arrested every do-it-yourself medical practitioner." I looked directly at Brenda. "I would have told you that last night if you'd given me the chance."

She almost spat her answer. "Then why didn't you leave it alone? Why did you have to do this, turn a spotlight on Antoinette's troubles?"

"I told you," I said stubbornly. "I had to know the truth."

"Very interesting indeed." Greathead wore what I considered a most unpleasant smile. "I'd followed the news stories, of course, and then, as I said, I made some calls last night. Knute is correct, Miss Evers. It would be most difficult to convict you of anything, but it was necessary to get at the truth."

Brenda was taken aback. "Why? Tell me why."

"Zelinda Pendleton is attempting to overturn her ex-husband's last will and testament," Greathead answered. "The man that's handling the case for her is an ac-quaintance of mine. In his opinion, she has a good chance to do just that. Unless you admit that the Clements baby is Pendleton's son, that might put a very different light on what seems to be a capricious will. I presume that you have acceptable proof. If you believe that the child is en-titled to his father's estate, and I assume you do, then your course is clear. Your niece is mentally ill, Brenda tells me. Would it injure her less to continue to deny the parentage? Of course, it's your decision and my brother attorney may be overly optimistic, you can never tell what a court will do. But my advice is to put the thing right out on the table. Today's world is not so apt to point a finger of scorn. It's no longer considered beyond the pale to bring a child into the world without benefit of clergy."

Antoinette set her mouth. "In Vale, it is."

"But if she proved parentage, couldn't Antoinette be accused of aiding and abetting Pendleton's death?" Brenda worried.

"By whom?" I asked. "I can just hear Granger when

he reads my report. Moses on the mountain, Knute, you know we can't touch this. Not with a ten-foot pole, that's what he'll say."

"You're gambling with a million dollars," Greathead told Antoinette. "I'll be happy to handle the legal side of it for you. As a favor, as I said, to my favorite secretary." He smiled smugly at Brenda.

"Ex-secretary," I reminded him.

"Knute." Antoinette folded her small hands in her lap. "I'd like to speak to you privately."

Greathead's eyebrows rose. He laughed and put out his cigar in the ashtray. "Come, my dear," he invited Brenda, "you can give me a cup of coffee in the kitchen. The cab driver who brought me here said nothing was open and I haven't had any breakfast. Perhaps I can convince you to return to my employ. Surely you must find domestic duties on the dull side by this time."

They left me seething.

"Knute, could we go out and sit in your car?" asked Antoinette. I'd almost forgotten about her for a minute.

"In my car? Sure." What on earth did she want to say to me? Something so private she didn't want to tell it even in her own living room? We walked out without speaking, but I was listening. All I could hear from the kitchen was a murmur of voices.

Out in the car, Antoinette reached over and touched my arm lightly. "Brenda is angry at you at this moment," she told me. "But she'll get over it. It's just that she's fond of me. And Doreen. Family loyalty, you understand."

I nodded. "I know. If I could have, I'd have let it alone. But I'm not made that way. I don't like to live with pretense. Secrets. Things that can't be brought out into the open."

"Out in the open." She removed her hand from my arm and brushed the back of it across her mouth as though that part of her face hurt her. "What a luxury. To have things out in the open. I wish I could afford it."

"I know. I saw the girl—she's enough to break anybody's heart. Why in hell didn't you make him marry her? Even if it wasn't ideal, it would have been better than this. Surely you knew her well enough to know her pressure points."

She nodded sadly. "Oh, I knew. When I found out about the baby—dear Jesus, then I found out! I didn't even know she'd been seeing him. She'd been introduced to him out at the roadhouse one night, she was there with a bunch of friends, it's one of the few places in town to go in the evening. Well, for the first time in her life she lied to me. I suppose he must have told her, don't tell your aunt, she'd never permit it. Well, he was right there! She was completely infatuated, she'd never known anyone like him before. Always boys before. Young men with no finesse who looked at her with awe and got tongue-tied. But this was a man, a charming man when he wanted to be, a famous man. How could she resist him? Even I could understand that."

"You found out after he'd left Vale?"

"On February fourteenth. Valentine's Day!" Her laugh was harsh and old. "I'll never forget it, never. The first thing that flashed into my mind was what could I do to make this man suffer? She cried, said she wanted to marry him, said if he knew he would come back and marry her. I said no, never, it would never work out, it was impossible. She said she'd marry him anyway, she'd write him and go to him and I said she couldn't possibly do that. And all the while, my brain was churning, looking for a way, a plot to cause him the same kind of pain he had caused me, the deep scarifying misery that filled the stomach with acid, that twisted the heart, that numbed the brain . . ."

I started to interrupt, but she went on. "It wasn't until after the baby was born that I came up with it. The punishment to fit the crime—the one way to hit him where it would hurt most." Her eyes blazed.

"Where was the baby born?"

"At the sanitarium. The founder was a close friend of my father's and though he's retired, he was still able to help me. They've been kind there. When the baby was born, there was something wrong with him . . ." I nodded that I knew. "I knew it would be difficult to find adoptive parents because of this, but I knew Pam Cragmore would help."

"You're saying that Doreen had her breakdown before the birth of the child?"

She turned her face to me, but I'm not sure she saw me. Her eyes suddenly brimmed with tears. "Oh, yes. She had it when I told her why she couldn't marry him. Under any circumstances." The tears welled over, began to fall. "Oh, what a dreadful old woman I am!" She moved her head so that I couldn't watch her cry.

Brenda came to the front door of the house, watched us for a moment, turned away. "Here," I said and handed Antoinette my handkerchief.

She blew her nose hard and I asked, "How did you convince him that he had syphilis?" That was the question that bugged me the most.

Muffled tones, "I told him that Doreen had had his child, that she and the child had been diseased, that she was in a mental hospital because of it, that the child had something wrong with him. Then I borrowed some stationery from my old doctor friend and I forged a letter corroborating my story. I said in it that he had no doubt infected himself, told him that he must have treatment immediately. In medical language I wrote that it wouldn't show up for a while, then I told him how it would be when it did. Vivid descriptions copied from one of my father's old medical books. I even included a pamphlet released to doctors and I signed my old friend's name. Arthur believed me. He even began to imagine early symptoms."

A letter from a doctor. Enough to put the fear of God into any man. And yet, if he'd only checked up on it . . . "Pendleton was unhinged on the subject." I was speaking to myself.

"Oh, yes, he was, but that was all to the good. I knew he'd never have the courage or the sense to go for treatment. I knew he'd believe me. He'd never known me to lie." She stressed the word known. "And it worked as I knew it would. When he telephoned me, pleaded with me to do him one favor, to get hold of the arsphenamine and bring it to the conference in Boston, I knew. He'd tried to get it himself, he said, he was close to whining, how that pleased me! He'd tried in some big California drugstore but there was a young man on duty, he'd never heard of arsphenamine and he called the senior pharmacist . . . well, Arthur ran, literally ran out of the place. He admitted it. After all his big talk of bravery, courage, inner strength!"

I backtracked, there were so many questions I had to ask. "And you told him where the child was—why? Why did you go to the trouble to get that information from your old friend Miss Cragmore and pass it on?"

"I hoped it would bother him. It's one thing to know you have a child somewhere, but not know where—and quite another to have the knowledge. To know where to go to see him, a terrible temptation, I should think. I could imagine he might promise himself he wouldn't want to see his child, but be drawn, irresistibly drawn . . . besides, the Clementses aren't wealthy. The baby will need medical treatment. I reasoned that Arthur couldn't sit by and let his own child be in want. And I was right about that!" Triumphantly, "He did leave them his money."

I was off on my own train of thought. "But I still don't understand why you wouldn't allow her to marry him. Even if he wouldn't, surely you could have persuaded him for the child's sake. He must have cared something about the child to make that will."

She sniffled. "That's what I brought you out here to tell you. Under no circumstances could I permit that —and I was afraid she'd run away to him, so I had to tell her."

Her voice sounded very different, I'd never heard her use this tone before. "Tell her what?"

"In 1951 I was at Weston College for Women, Alumni secretary." Her voice changed again, she was acting a part. "A promising young writer was a guest lecturer there, Arthur Glenn Pendleton. I was forty, an old maid. He was thirty, a young bachelor. For some reason known only to him, he took it upon himself to seduce the old maid. Doreen is his child and mine."

"Good God in heaven." I spoke reverently.

"I didn't love him, I didn't want him, but I wanted the child. I resigned from the college, came to my brother

Forrest. He and his wife agreed we'd say Doreen was theirs, a child of the menopause. That's what we did and I saw her every day, helped raise her. Later, when they passed away, she naturally came to live with me. No one ever knew, not Doreen, not even Arthur. I would never give him the satisfaction."

"My God," I swore again. "He didn't know . . . you never told . . ." The thought flashed through my mind that that confession would have changed the lives of several people—Pendleton, Doreen, the child, Antoinette herself. "Did you hate him so much twenty years ago?" I asked slowly.

She closed her eyes briefly, opened them again. "I don't remember. I don't remember what I felt for him. Only that the child was mine, that he was to have no part of it. I knew he cared nothing for me—I'd been used as a mother confessor. The place, the time, I was the person he'd unburdened his soul to. I suppose everyone needs to do that, once if never again. And having trusted me with his weaknesses, he detested me for knowing. All this I knew, pondered during the long agonizing nights as the baby grew and grew." She covered her face with one small hand.

After a moment, she took her hand away. "And so—having made my bed with dirty linen, I had to lie in it. And then I found, like mother, like daughter. The mills of the gods grind exceedingly small."

"Where did you get the arsphenamine?"

Again, the hooded eyes. "I won't tell you that. It was an innocent favor. There's no need to involve anyone else."

"But what did you think—when he asked you for it?"

A small sigh. "It was as though I'd written the story. I thought my plan had worked, that he was suffering as I had intended. He was in hell along with me."

I had to know. "Did you mean the medicine to kill him?"

She studied my eyes. "I'll try to be honest. I don't know. But I think I hoped it would. Yes, I know I hoped it would."

I didn't know what to say. There was nothing I could say except, sincerely, "I'm sorry. Damned sorry. I should have let it lay. Brenda was right."

"I'd prefer, in fact I beg you . . . please don't let anyone else know. Ever. Not even for the sake of the money could I bear . . . when I told Doreen . . . well, you saw what happened. If she doesn't get well . . . I've been punished about as much as any human being can be punished and live."

"You have my word," I promised solemnly. "Not even my wife."

"Thank you." She smiled tremulously, for the moment a girl again. "I like you, Knute. Welcome to the family, the rest of it's all right. And, Knute, there's one other thing. Don't be angry at Brenda. There's something she'll be telling you herself and perhaps I shouldn't say it first, but just once in my life I'd like to be the bearer of good tidings. Brenda's going to have a baby."

The wind was tearing at the balcony doors but inside the apartment all was warm and cozy. Brenda sat knitting, Mein curled up beside her. Very domestic, very pregnant, very beautiful.

I said, "Did you see in the paper? Pendleton's posthumous book got a great review."

"I've read the book, just finished it. I was lucky enough to get a copy at the library."

"It says it's about a young writer and an older woman. They say it's a sensitive love story."

"Anything new on Zelinda Pendleton's suit?" Brenda came to the end of a knitted row, turned her needles. The yarn was yellow, the rows were short.

"She's appealed it. Greathead himself called me to say so far so good for the Clementses."

"Did he? That's nice." Only polite interest.

"She didn't plan to kill him," I said suddenly. I'd been wanting to tell her that for days.

"Antoinette?" My wife looked at me gravely.

"I've figured it out. If she'd meant to, she wouldn't have hung around after she gave him the arsphenamine. Wouldn't have made all that fuss, called the maid and all if she'd meant him to die. All she had to do was go away and let him be."

"Poor Antoinette. How she must have hated him." She finished another row, turned the needles. She knitted quickly.

"Uhmmm," I answered.

"Only—in the book . . ."

"Yes?"

"Maybe it wasn't autobiographical at all, but it reads as though . . ."

"As though what?"

"As though they loved each other very much once. The writer and the older woman."

The balcony door blew open and wind drew sleet in. I hurried to fasten it, lock it. I shivered. "It's going to be a bastard of a winter."

"Oh, I don't know," said Brenda placidly. "It won't be so bad. Spring will be here before we know it."

I looked down at her bent head. "What will we name him?"

"Her." She looked up, eyes dancing.

"Him—her. Whatever."

"Knute, Junior?"

I leaned over, kissed the top of her head. "Not on your tintype. Thanks, but no thanks."

"I'm going to get a book on names," she spoke thoughtfully. "So we'll know what they mean."

"Mean?"

"Uh-huh. I'm going to see if there's a name that means child of the truth seeker."

I straightened up. "That sounds—damned presumptuous. Am I that stuffy?"

Brenda dropped her knitting, reached up to me. "Oh, no, darling. Just terribly honest. A priceless legacy—better than any old million dollars any day."

I pulled her up, spoke into her hair. "We'll name him George after my father."

"Darling," sighed Brenda, "I really don't care for that name. I love your father, but—George!"

"Shut up," I said and kissed her. Kissed years of future arguments right on her sexy mouth. Fifty years, if I was lucky. And I was lucky.

The cat woke up, got down on the floor and began to unravel the fallen knitting. I saw him do it but didn't say anything. Brenda was a fast knitter. She could start all over again tomorrow.